wiccan
wisdomkeepers

Wiccan wisdomkeepers

Modern-Day Witches Speak on Environmentalism, feminism, Motherhood, Wiccan Lore, and More

Text and Photography by
sally griffyn

WEISERBOOKS
Boston, MA/York Beach, ME

This book is dedicated to the Witches in this book who dare to walk the path of the wise.
Special thanks to Justina, Jane and Debbie for their practical help in the creation of this book.

First published in the United States in 2002 by
Red Wheel/Weiser, LLC
368 Congress Street
Boston, MA 02210
www.redwheelweiser.com

First published 2002 under the title
Wiccan Wisdomkeepers by Godsfield Press Ltd.,
Godsfield House, Old Alresford, Hants, SO24 9RQ.

Text and photography copyright © Sally Griffyn.

Book copyright © Godsfield Press.

The right of Sally Griffyn to be identified as the author of this work has been asserted by her accordance with the UK Copyright Designs and Patents Act 1988.

The text on pages 118-119 is excerpted from *WitchCrafting: A Spiritual Guide to Making Magic* (Broadway Books, 2001/HarperCollins UK 2002)

The publisher would like to thank Fleur Fitzgerald for permission to use the photograph on page 15 and Sirona Knight for the photographs on pages 134, 135, and 138.

Cataloging-in-Publication Data available on request from the Library of Congress.

Weiser Books ISBN: 1-57863-257-9

Printed in China

Editor: Jane Alexander
Designer: Justina Leitão

09 08 07 06 05 04 03 02

8 7 6 5 4 3 2 1

CONTENTS

INTRODUCTION
A PERSPECTIVE ON WICCA

At the dawn of the new millennium, many spiritual traditions think that the twenty-first century will be a Golden Age, with tremendous shifts of consciousness on a universal scale. The spiritual knowledge of older religions is being sought as an answer to the overwhelming pace of modern life. There has been a tendency for the West to seek inspiration from the East, as Western patriarchal religions do not encourage the direct experience of the divine, nor do they consider nature and the environment. However, the growing interest in the ancient lore of the Celts has proliferated in one particular tradition, Wicca. Although Wicca is the modern branch of a much older nature religion, Wise Craft or Witchcraft, it offers some ancient insights from Western sources. Many teachings that have been hidden and almost forgotten are now being revisited and, indeed, reinvented. The resurgence in interest in the land as teacher has moved into focus for those interested in British Pagan history.

The Witchcraft Law was repealed in Britain in 1951, and since then Witches in Britain have benefited from a legal system that supports their right to follow their spiritual path. Much of the available work on Witchcraft has been published within the last few decades as Wiccan pioneers have opened their hearts and written about the mystery religion that is the Craft. To become an initiated Witch it is necessary to swear oaths of secrecy. These were imposed for good reason—someone calling themselves a Witch is open to persecution even today.

Wiccans cover a broad spectrum of men and women practicing various healing arts. Wicca is a spiritual path that worships a male and female form of the divine known as the Goddess and the Horned God. The Goddess is the land and the seasons, and is known as Aradia and by many other names. The God is the wild force of nature once known as the Green Man, John Barley Corn, and Old Horny. The teachings form a body of lore that speaks of the land as alive and encourages the direct experience of deity. At its heart is the reverence for nature as immanent deity, teacher, and bringer of all spiritual wisdom. Witches are both part of the cycle of living and observers in that cycle, for Witches act as a medium to this flow. Many Wiccans are concerned about our relationship with the land and are active environmentalists. The teachings are nondogmatic and are governed by the tenet "an it harm none, do what thou wilt."

Right: Offering a chalice of wine, symbolic of spiritual wisdom and the blood of life.

Hand-carved wands made of the wood of different trees. Each tree has various qualities associated with it. The wand is one of the Witches tools and represents the element of Fire and will power.

Both men and women are Wiccans, and come from most stratas of society. Nevertheless, it can be said that it is a religion represented primarily by white, middle-class people. Many are academics. They practice in temples as simple as a living room, or in elaborate rooms used only for ritual, outside in all weathers, on hills and in woods. Many dance and chant at ancient sacred sites so as to follow in the footprints of their ancestors. The "Craft," as it is known, is loosely bonded in ethics but is frequently practiced quite differently from coven to coven, and from country to country.

A coven is a group of working Witches and traditionally has no more than thirteen members. It is said that the number thirteen holds particular significance, as it is the number of moons in a year, and therefore honors the cyclical Goddess of nature. A number with a moon connection is considered to be a Goddess number and therefore historically was thought to be lucky. As with most ideas attacked by the church, the misrepresentation of this number as one of "bad luck" is evidence of the effectiveness of the propaganda by the incoming Christian Church against native religions.

The number also holds importance in terms of managing community decisions. Small groups of like-minded people are able to make effective decisions and work in harmony with each other. Raising the number

Magic is always an act of intention. It is the will to change for the better; the energy to help when all seems futile; it is prayer; and it is potent focused energy. It can speed up healing or slow down illness. It can bend and shift what is only possibility into the manifestation of dreams. If the universe lends an ear, then Witches are the whisperers who breathe life into action.

in the group above thirteen tends to change the profile of the group.

The purpose of the gathering is to celebrate the wheel of the year, honor the gods and goddesses of the land, and to work the magic of transformation. Magic is an act of intention. It is the will to change for the better; the energy to help when all seems futile; it is prayer; and it is potent focused energy. It can speed up healing or slow down illness. It can bend and shift what is only possibility into the manifestation of dreams. If the universe lends an ear, then Witches are the whisperers who breathe life into action. When a child is ill, Witches will raise and send energy and the group may ask for that little bit of help that makes a difference. They may work from a distance and they may be be on the front line, offering help in hospices and on conservation projects in the local community.

The form that magic takes is always decided by the coven, which decides how best to send energy to a particular situation. Healing has to be requested before magical intervention takes place, as it would be considered

Crystal gazing or scrying is one of the Witch's methods of foretelling the future. This method of divination may reveal the inner workings of a situation.

unethical to perform healing without permission. Energy can be raised in a number of traditional methods: by repeating mantras or rhyming verse, known as spellcraft; trance; dance; meditation; visualization; and drumming to name a few. The energy is then sent to the ill person, either by physically holding them, or it is put psychically into a talisman for the person to wear.

Besides this kind of magic there is also the magic of transformation. If someone is suffering in an unhappy relationship, they may require inner transformation to release themselves from the situation. Coven members will not only provide the practical support and listen to the person in

A pentacle marked with the eight Celtic festivals which mark the Wiccan calendar and celebrate the seasonal cycle of the year.

Matthew Hopkins, the notorious Witchfinder General. He was paid to "find" Witches in rural English villages and was responsible for torturing terrified villagers and extracting confessions. Here, a woman confesses to having several "familiars," animals who helped her do evil deeds.

need of help, but also, rather than meddle in a situation, they will send that person energy so they are able to do what is best for themselves. There is a great adage: be careful what you ask for because it will come true. This is always borne in mind when making decisions about magical work, for it is believed that every sentient being has a path to walk and lessons to learn in their own way and time. What can be done is to help release negative emotions and to create feelings of well being on that path.

Historically, Witches have been maligned, and the wicked Witch is always the "bad guy" in the story. In fact many fairy tales are Christian warnings of the dangers of running off with the fairies, for they represent the remnants of the pre-Christian Pagan folk. There is much evidence to suggest that fairies and Witches in stories and myth are the native peoples of Britain, who practiced a simple, earth-based, spirituality. The terms are now weighed down with hundreds of years of propaganda. It is much rarer to hear of the "good" witch in children's fairy tales. In recent

years the Harry Potter books and other inventive creations are changing some of those perceptions, but the media has not been kind to Pagans. Historically, Witches suffered the most brutal repression at the hands of the Christian Church in Europe.

The infamous Spanish Inquisition and, in Britain, the Witchfinder General, tore through remote villages, torturing those who threatened the patriarchal misogynist establishment. It resulted in a period of history called the "burning times," which has

no definite beginning or end. Certainly it ranged from the early medieval period until the late seventeenth century. Even after that period "Witches" suffered many forms of abuse, including alienation from the community, public humiliation (shaving the head, being placed in stocks and having eggs and rotten fruit thrown at them), and being brought in front of Church elders for condemnation. The infamous Witch testing, which was designed to unearth potential Witches from the God-fearing community, also included impossible tests. In one of these, known as "swimming a Witch," the individual was tied by the arms and feet to a long rope and dropped into a pond or river. Although the binding prevented any attempts at swimming anyway, the law said that if the individual sank and was received by the water (a symbol of Godliness) they were not a Witch; if they swam, they were rejected by the water and were therefore guilty of Witchcraft. If the latter, the Witch would be tortured, tried, and hanged.

During the most intense period, anyone who was thought to pose a

The Museum of Witchcraft in Boscastle, Cornwall, which hosts a huge collection of authentic Witchcraft items, is now owned by Graham King (pictured).

A medieval Woodcut depicts "swimming a Witch." If she swam it was proof of Witchcraft; if she sank she was innocent. Was it better to drown innocent, than swim and be hanged or burned as a Witch?

threat was systematically murdered to the cry "burn the Witch." In Europe they burned them and in England and America they hanged them. The number of those accused from medieval times to the eighteenth century is estimated to be in the region of six million. We have no idea how many were killed but small reminders of the cruelty inflicted still exist. At the base of Edinburgh castle there is a little plaque commemorating the two thousand people burned as Witches on pyres within the castle walls.

Women were the primary targets for this repression, which helped keep the patriarchal Christian religion in control. Also affected were herbalists, medicine women, disabled women, ugly women, beautiful women, men-loving Witches, men-loving men, women-loving women, women and men with property, women in power, adulterous women, midwives, fortune tellers, mentally handicapped people, dissidents, political opponents, seductive women, women who liked sex, and hermits.

Even the terms we use now have been corrupted. Pagan meant "rustic or rural dweller." Heathen meant "men of the heaths." The word "Witch" has

> Behind the masks of the God and Goddess is the universal energy that is neither male nor female.

the same etymological root as "wise." Many who suffered were not even actively practicing the old religion but were caught in the fervor of religious zeal meted out by some men in power.

Now, in the twenty-first century, people can speak freely about the Old Religion and it calls to those seeking the spirit of the land. Women and men who wish to see active representations of a female deity find that Wicca, if not resolving all imbalances, certainly points to a female-centered, compassionate, nurturing, spiritual path. The image of the all-loving, all-powerful, changeless and eternal, sexually courageous Goddess who inhabits the world of myth and the imagination speaks to the post-modern sensibility. In Wicca there are also powerful representations of the God: an image of the compassionate, potent, benevolent, and unashamedly sexual male.

Behind the masks of the God and Goddess is the universal energy that is neither male nor female. In fact the universal force behind all rites in Wicca is Nature.

The wheel of the year is the seasonal cycle representing the Witches calendar. Rituals mark each significant turn and as all seasons have their own distinctive mood and atmosphere, the ritual reflects the time of year. Nature as teacher activates the Wiccan imagination in the form of seasonal festivities and teachings. These are the eight Celtic rites, four of which are solar and four agricultural. The solar rites are Midwinter, Midsummer, and the two Equinoxes. Midwinter marks the the longest night, when the sun is farthest from the earth. Midsummer marks the longest day, when the sun is nearest to the earth. At the Spring and Autumn Equinoxes the days and nights are of equal length.

The other four ritual nights are perhaps more ancient and are rooted in mythology. May Eve, or Beltane (30 April), is the traditional love or

A Wiccan priestess standing in the hollow of an oak tree. Witches revere nature and the life force of the land.

fertility festival. A time of abundant growth and flowering, with sexuality at its height, many rites this night are for lovers. Lammas, or Lughnasagh (1 August), is the harvest festival; it is the time to cut the crop and store it safely away. There is an element of sacrifice, of gathering in the ripeness of life. Nothing will remain at its peak. Symbolically, this is a good time to let go of some things in order to keep the best of the crop.

Halloween, or Samhain (31 October), is the Celtic New Year, when the rite of the waning year is celebrated. It is the feast of death and with it the understanding that in the cycle of rebirth, the trees shed their leaves that they may return in spring. Death here is seen as a rest period that is necessary

May Day is the traditional love festival of the Wiccan calendar. Women dress in May greenery to celebrate in this local gathering on the Welsh borders.

for the return of life the following year. And as nature reveals her cycle, so Witches call the names of loved ones who have died during the previous year. They are remembered and may be invited to cross the veil.

The return of the light and the breaking of the period of rest is celebrated at Imbolc, or Candlemass (2 February). At this time, which is still very much winter, the light is coming back and days are getting longer. This is a good time for new ideas and to start new projects.

Interwoven into this continuous cycle is the monthly moon cycle, which brings awareness of the rising and falling of the tides, the emotions, the passions, and the growth of plants. Witches work magic into the fabric of the seasons and the monthly

moon cycles: sun and moon and earth are in harmony. There are times for growing, times for creating, and times for removing obstacles and letting go. Everything has its appropriate moment. The understanding of these cycles is essential to the Craft, so that those initiated into the teachings can work magic.

The Wiccan lore is handed down from teacher to pupil and each initiate creates their own handwritten *Book of Shadows*. The lore is mostly a compilation of Gerald Gardner's teachings, with Doreen Valiente's additions and seasonal rites. It is part recipe and spell book, part sound advice, poetry, and words of wisdom. Gardner's *Book of Shadows* was published in the 1950s, and for many was the catalyst to undergo Wiccan training. Called

The Green Man is the Pagan God of Life and growth. Craftsmen worked Pagan themes into the masonry of churches and many are found carved in the ceilings of churches. This is a modern rendition by Fleur Fitzgerald.

Interwoven into this continuous cycle is the monthly moon cycle, which brings awareness of the rising and falling of the tides, the emotions, the passions and the growth of plants. Witches work magic into the fabric of the seasons and the monthly moon cycles: sun and moon and earth are in harmony. There are times for growing, times for creating, times for removing obstacles and letting go.

The stones of Stenness in the Orkney Islands, Scotland. According to oral tradition, Neolithic sacred sites are connected with Witches and Pagans. They are the ancestral ritual sites of the British Isles that predate the influx of Christianity.

Gardnerian Wicca, after its founder, it established a system of training akin to the apprenticeship of a craftsman. Initiation into the Craft was a step into the unknown, and the initiate had to take an oath of secrecy. The supplicant had to show an interest in an often hidden path. Doreen Valiente remarked how difficult it was to find information about Witchcraft—it was Gardner's association with the Museum of Witchcraft that enabled her to contact someone in the Craft.

Gardner had come across a coven in the New Forest. The High Priestess, Dorothy Clutterbuck, initiated him into an unbroken line of traditional Witches. He initiated Doreen, and others with her help. Gardner wanted to make Witchcraft available to others and to this end published *High Magic's Aid*, a supposedly fiction title. It essentially maps out the secret path of the Witch and tells the story of the Craft. Gardner went public and enabled others to do so by challenging

> **Initiation into the Craft was a step into the unknown, and the initiate had to take an oath of secrecy.**

outdated laws. It resulted in the repeal of the 1951 Witchcraft Law.

First degree made a man or woman a Witch in name and they were shown some tools and learnt some ritual teachings. The commitment to be a

Witch was in effect the agreement to train with a coven and to learn the seasonal festivals. Second degree involved a deeper study and the commitment to serve the children of Wise Craft. A second degree was sufficiently versed in Craft to be able to pass on the traditions accurately, and could initiate others. The third degree is still reserved for those who have both shown commitment and run a coven. In Gardnerian covens, second and third degree were taken simultaneously and required no more than a year and a day's training in first. Later, covens trained for longer. It is not unusual now in Alexandrian and Gardenerian covens to take more than ten years of training to reach this level. If the individual is not actively running a coven they may be initiated into the third degree if they have proved themselves to their elders.

The third degree involves the Great Rite, which is the individual's union with God or Goddess, depending upon the gender of the initiate. Women are initiated by a third-degree male and men by a third-degree female. Traditionally, regardless of their

A Wiccan holding two symbols of Witchcraft—the besom or broom and the staff. Brooms represent thresholds and in the Handfasting, or Wiccan marriage ceremony, the couple jump the broom, entering the new life together. The staff is symbolic of the potency of the male in phallic form.

sexual orientation, individuals are initiated by a member of the opposite sex to bring the knowledge of union with a fertile principle.

Wicca is both a fertility cult and a polar current so the universal concept of birth into a different state is represented by a male and female. In the third degree, if an initiate is working with their partner, the rite will be consecrated with lovemaking. If not, then the Great Rite will be symbolic only. Initiations are always a rite of passage in which the initiate undertakes a rigorous set of challenges and

The pentacle, symbol of the four elements—Earth, Air, Fire and Water—with Spirit at the top.

The Winter Solstice rite of the New York Faeries, a political ritual gay group who hold large rituals on eight Celtic festivals. The altar is lit with candles to represent the coming of the light on the longest night of the year.

is shown mysteries, and is a process of self-transformation. The change is akin to the birth of a new self.

Nowadays the idea that opposite sexes should be part of the rite has been challenged by those outside the heterosexual construct. Women who do not wish to be initiated by men and are members of Dianic covens (named after the virgin goddess, Diana), symbolically represent union with the divine differently, as do gay covens. Solitary Witches have of necessity reconstructed union with the divine. Gardner was of his time and was homophobic. If Wicca is to uphold its attitude as non-dogmatic, it has to encompass different symbols of the divine. Many now agree that nature,

being genderless, must be represented as aspects of both genders. Masculine and feminine symbols are within everyone symbolically.

Wicca was, and is, a religion based on community. Small groups of people form covens and when the coven gets too big—sometimes literally for a nine-foot circle to accommodate all the members—some would hive off. The family of Witches would then be linked with a group mind but impart its differences and take on the personality of the High Priest and High Priestess. This ensures that each group works by general consensus and also reflects the interests of the people involved. Some covens, like Gardner's first coven, are filled with practical people who are skilled at making tools and other ritual items. Gardner was a jewelry maker and created many beautiful ritual items. Doreen Valiente can be seen wearing the silver bracelet that Gardner made for her third degree on page 37. He also made charms and brooches of flying Witches that are now in the Museum of Witchcraft in Cornwall.

As he was a great believer in naturism, the coven members would meet and hold their rites naked or "sky-clad." This, and the fact that Witches revere nature as unashamedly sexual, is the root of some of the misrepresentations of Wiccans as sexually obsessed and holding orgies. In fact the naked body is seen as natural and beautiful, and is honored as an expression of nature. Removing clothes also removes the obvious inequalities of rank and status, and to be free as on the day you were born shows great reverence for the divine in human form.

Gardner himself was a member of a naturist club that worked to ensure that the right to naturism was maintained, and his coven met in the club-house of his local naturist club. Wiccans have a high regard for nature and human sexuality and consensual sex between partners is considered a divine act. As Doreen Valiente's "Charge of the Goddess" states: "all acts of love and pleasure are my rituals." This has led to speculation about Wicca's relationship to sexuality. In some rites a couple may make love as part of the celebrations. This is always consensual. This celebration of sexuality is very different from Christian morality. Gardner's own prejudice is revealed in his infamous "Laws," which included anti-homosexual sentiments. In effect he suggested that

A Witch charm or protection talisman from the Witchcraft Museum.

A chalice used in a Handfasting, or Wiccan wedding. The couple being joined drink from the chalice for health and love.

A Wiccan High Priestess in a ritual position, with arms crossed.

Wicca could only be a magical path for hetero-sexuals; many groups have since attacked this stance. In her speech to the Pagan Federation in 1997, Doreen Valiente attempted to put right this injustice when she spoke on behalf of gay relations in the Craft. She said that in all probability Gardner had written the Laws himself and had not, as he inferred, found them as part of an ancient text. She also took issue with the idea that the High Priestess should always be young so as the represent a fertile goddess, which she considered misogynist. Gardner was going public in a time when many could lose their jobs if known to be involved in Witchcraft, and it was this, and other issues, that led to Doreen's break with Gardner's coven. However, she stayed in touch with Gerald and always spoke of him with great respect.

Another Witch who greatly influenced the history and development of the Craft was Alex Sanders, at one time known as the "King of the Witches." He claimed to have been initiated by his grandmother and have family ties to an ancient line of British Witches. He came to the fore in the 1960s, with his wife Maxine. Sanders emphasized ritual magic and formal ceremony. Whereas Gardner was more rustic, Sanders looked to Ancient Egyptian, Greek, and Roman mythology, and the Kabbala (the mystical teachings of Judaism). Alex was very good at training a large number of initiates quickly and he spawned many covens that

It has been difficult for researchers to find the roots of Wicca. It is true that Witchcraft is a shamanistic earth religion of the British Isles. This is reflected by the more primitive rites within the formal Craft, such as tree reverence, ecstatic dancing, moon worship, fire ritual, and the seasonal festivals. However, much of this ritual was created in the twentieth century.

hived off and multiplied. Sanders was also bisexual and so his ideas were in some ways part of the revolution of the 1960s and enabled the idea that all sexuality is divine to emerge in Wicca.

In Wicca there are a number of types of lineage; as well as Gardnerian and Alexandrian there are lines that come from traditional and hereditary Witches, and those shaped by the striking personality of the founder of a coven, such as Robert Cochrane. Doreen Valiente worked with this highly intelligent and mystical man, whose short life meant that he did not have the time to introduce as many to his form of Wise Craft. He is still held in immense regard. Doreen considered his large and intricate rituals to be part of an entirely different lineage, probably a hereditary one. He worked magic outside in the elements: high places and woodland for the God, and caves for the Goddess. He didn't use the titles High Priestess and High Priest in his rituals; rather he used the Lady and the Master, which seemed to Doreen to come from a different source, and possibly a very old one. Certainly there have been village

Witches who have passed down insights and herbal medicine to their offspring, but there is no known systematic training and grouping of people practicing devotion to the Old Gods. Many who say they are from hereditary lines do not speak about it further and their silence keeps their heritage a mystery.

The history of Witchcraft has been a hidden path, so it has been difficult for researchers to find the roots of this cult. It is true that Witchcraft is a shamanistic earth religion of the British Isles. This is reflected by the

Many ancient sacred wells were dedicated to a Goddess, often Brid, and offerings are still left, as at this well in Ireland. Though the icon is that of Mary, a Christian figure, she would have originally been the Great Goddess.

An eighteenth-century representation of a Witch. She has some of the traditional symbols of Witchcraft—the broom, the owl and the pointed hat.

The stone circle of Callanish in Lewes, in the Outer Hebrides. It is said that a Witch came here to milk a cow whose milk was never ending. Stone circles predate Christianity by thousands of years whereas Witchcraft was a much later earth-based spirituality. However, historically Witches have worshipped at these sites.

more primitive rites within the formal Craft, such as tree reverence, ecstatic dancing, moon worship, fire ritual, and the seasonal festivals. However, much of this formal ritual was created in the twentieth century by some of the figureheads mentioned above. As yet there is little known about the role of hereditary Witches—they seem to pass on folk knowledge such as healing charms and other ancient cures within their family. These rural remedies were a way of dealing with the uncertainty that life offers. In the Museum of Witchcraft there are some remarkable items that come from a period when it was the local wise women who would help the sick, pregnant women, and sick animals, and who would minister to the community in times of need. They fulfilled the important role that a psychologist or doctor fills today, and would listen and advise on matters of love and family. Interestingly, many modern Witches are also psycholo-

> *The local wise women would help pregnant women and the sick, and would minister to the community.*

gists, such as Judy Harrow (*see* pages 96-103), who has written about group dynamics in Wicca.

All communities inevitably have to deal with hardships, and the Witch as advisor offered a valuable service, for instance by offering counsel to a woman who was being beaten by a man. There are many historical reports of a wise woman or man helping people with what would now be called psychological disturbances. Those in power, historically men, would often then accuse the Witch of interfering in their marriage and then provoke a campaign of abuse. In these cases the local wise folk sometimes defended themselves by creating a charm that could be used to intimidate a malicious neighbor. Although the tenet of Wicca in the twentieth century is "an it harm none, do what thou wilt," historically there are many instances where Witches were accused of practicing the "black arts."

Polmadrone Dolmen in County Clare, Ireland, is a Neolithic burial chamber.

(a doll made of wax or cloth), which could be stuck with pins to strike the accuser ill. Like the famous voodoo dolls, these could offer a psychological defense for a woman whose life was in danger but also could create fear in the community. In all religions there are those who misuse power, and some old curses were indeed used to send ill intent.

Poppets were also created to send healing. They use a very old system of sympathetic magic in which the image of the person who is ill is healed from a distance with the power of will. The dolls also have been used to protect a home.

Healing rites have long been a central act of Wise Craft, and many of the Witches in this book refer to them. Dawn Hardy, who was initiated by Alex Sanders, gives a simple spell which she used used to help a child who had been bullied. Traditional poppets sometimes would have had the hair of the ill person attached to them, but Dawn uses a more direct and modern representation of the person in need—a photograph. Obtaining something personal of the

Often a woman was accused of Witchcraft after an event was misinterpreted, or after an unfortunate coincidence, such as a cow becoming ill after a particular woman milked her. The accused woman frequently consulted the cunning woman of the village for advice on how to defend herself. She may have made a poppet

person they are doing magic for helps focus the intent, and it also enables the coven to meet and raise healing energy without the person being there. Linking the group mind with an object connected to the person makes the magic more effective.

Other Wiccans speak about the magic of transformation, in which the main focus of the rites is to heal the earth or to affect positive transforma-

tion on themselves. Francesca Howell represents a line of Wiccans who make a pledge to work for the preservation and conservation of the earth. Her political and spiritual interests intertwine: she not only works magic to heal the earth but also has been actively involved in Greenpeace and other organizations who fight for the

preservation of the rainforests and endangered species. Francesca has campaigned for human rights as well as animal and earth rights.

Starhawk is another politically motivated Wiccan. She has moved from the active role of teaching Wicca to teaching political activists magical techniques for engaging in peaceful protest. Her activities have combined the use of transformation magic in the face of globalization. She too is on the front line and has been using methods learned in the anti-war protests of the 1960s to empower young people. Her recent work included using imagery to unite protesters during the Seattle and G8 summits in 2001. By weaving ancient images into the tapestry of their work, the

Some of Alex Sanders' ritual tools and his athame. The athame is the Witch's knife, and is used to direct energy, not to cut. It is a symbol of the element of Air.

Standing stones of Callanish known as the maid, mother, and crone. The triple Goddess is mentioned throughout Europe and the British Isles and represents the changing face of woman. The stones constitute a potent symbol of Witchcraft.

protesters creatively invoke Goddesses to represent the transformation needed. The image of the Spider Goddess was used in Quebec; women tied rags that had been "charged" with energy into the fences that held protesters out of the discussions. Their intent was to highlight the worldwide economic inequality of women workers, seamstresses who, like the spider, are weavers, making cloth for multinational companies. The hard edges of the fencing was broken with soft rags and cloths—symbolic acts link the politics with the magical intent.

Male Wiccans are not adequately represented in this book. However, the three who do speak are deeply involved in Witchcraft and have been for many years. Edmund, who writes under a pseudonym, addresses the issues that compel him to keep his anonymity and the place of men in Wicca. He also provides great insights into the inner workings of a coven. He is an expert in the history of Paganism and Witchcraft in Britain, and he explores both the ancient roots of Witchcraft and its development in the twentieth century.

Tony Meadows discusses his long-term relationship with Wicca and with the woman who is his High Priestess and partner. Together, Dawn and Tony

speak of the power of a magical relationship. They come from a mixed Gardnerian/Alexandrian lineage and blend their different styles of Craft to produce their own kind of Wicca, which they then pass on to their initiates. Tony and Dawn are not alone when they relate how deeply they are influenced by location and how this shapes the way magic is worked.

Dawn and Tony's experience of practicing Wicca in the Welsh borders is very different from Phyllis Curott in Manhattan, Judy Harrow in New Jersey, and Janet Farrar and Gavin Bone in rural Ireland. Though the city dwellers have to work in temples in their homes, a reverence for nature is the essence of Wicca, so they are constantly in touch with the seasons and express their symbolic relationship to the land through ritual and magic.

Although the media continues to misrepresent Wicca, there are

Blessing the wine in a chalice. The Priest holds the chalice, a symbol of the feminine, and the Priestess holds the athame, symbol of the masculine.

stirrings afoot that suggest the return of the most important aspects of the ancient religion of the British Isles. Like any good native religion, Wise Craft went underground when under threat and, like preliterate teachings throughout the world, the lore remained part of an oral tradition.

A living tradition, Wicca, the modern version of Witchcraft, takes up the themes of the seasons, the cycle of the moon, God and Goddess as immanent in nature, healing from the land, and men and women working together on a spiritual path. The Wiccan Wisdomkeepers are those who have something to pass on and to bring forth from this dark history. They are connected by their love of the land and by a sense that as human beings we are responsible for our own destiny. The magic of transformation is conveyed in the chant, "she changes everything she touches, everything she touches, changes." Within this circle can be heard the voices of practicing Witches. They follow different traditions and have learned from various teachers. Some teach the Craft; others are the wise women of the village. They come to us from Ireland, Europe, Britain, and the United States. This book constitutes a global coven of people who sit like elders in council. Here Wiccans come together to share some of the secrets of the Craft. They are the Wiccan Wisdomkeepers.

> *They are connected by their love of the land and a sense that we are responsible for our own destiny.*

When creating a sacred circle, Wiccans honor the four elements. Here, Water is blessed on the altar.

Stonehenge, a temple to the sun, is still visited by modern Witches and Pagans. At summer solstice sunlight shines through the great lintels and strikes a shadow into the heart of this ancient sacred site.

DOREEN VALIENTE
"MOTHER OF WITCHCRAFT"

Doreen Valiente is still considered the "Mother of Witchcraft." Her long life, dedicated to the Old Religion, ended on 1 September 1999 at the ripe old age of 77. She was proud to be a Witch, lived as a Witch, and like a good Witch, died on the waning moon. Doreen was Gerald Gardner's High Priestess in the early 1950s; she split with the group over issues of publicity when he insisted on having young priestesses to represent the Goddess. In the 1960s she worked briefly with another famous Witch, Robert Cochrane, until his untimely death. For much of her later life, she stopped working with groups and worked ritual solely with her beloved partner and fellow Witch, Ron ("Cookie") Cooke.

Her influence on the present day Wiccan body of lore is so substantial that she undoubtedly can be considered the most influential woman in Wicca, and her *Witches' Book of Shadows* is a pre-eminent text. Her chants and invocations are recognizable for their rhythm and for their ability to induce trance states. The most famous text in Wicca is the 'Charge of the Goddess' (*see* page 41), which establishes the fundamental ideas upon which Wicca is based. Doreen was responsible for creating the present-day version of the Charge from early Pagan sources.

Doreen Valiente's last public speech at the Pagan Federation Conference, held in Croydon, England, in November 1997, received a standing ovation. Her notes for the address follow. They go a long way to explaining the views and beliefs she held at the end of her life, and answer many important questions about the history of Wicca and her view of its role in the twenty-first century.

Sub Rosa

Midsummer, and the chariot
Of the Sun
Pauses upon the height, a few fair days.
A stillness hangs in the enchanted air,
And breezes dance along the ancient ways.
Brief is the darkness, filled
With faint moonlight,
And rosy dawn its silent
Message brings
Of hope renewed, out of the
Deepest night,
And life and love, within the
Heart of things.
With summer comes the
Opening of the rose,
That without words,
Her secret can disclose.

DOREEN'S LAST POEM, 2 JULY 1999

The Museum of Witchcraft in Boscastle, Cornwall, England, is pictured on the left. Doreen Valiente was first attracted to Witchcraft by an article about this museum, then located on the Isle of Man.

"Friends, I stand here today accused of helping to found a new religion. As I have always believed that organized religion is nothing but a curse to humanity, this places me in a very embarrassing position. I am therefore grateful to the Pagan Federation for giving me this opportunity to defend myself from this serious charge.

"However, I think that what happened in 1951, when Gerald Gardner 'went public' about the survival of Witchcraft in Britain, was simply an example of the manifestation of an idea whose time had come. People like old Gerald and myself were simply the means through which it manifested, thanks to something which stirred upon the Inner Planes. Why, I don't know, but most probably something to do with the incoming of the Aquarian Age.

"It was in July 1951 that the Witches' Mill in Castletown, Isle of Man, was opened as a museum of Witchcraft, under the name of the Folklore Centre. The old Witches' Mill lit a beacon for Pagans and Witches everywhere. It was reading an article about this museum that first attracted me into Witchcraft. That is how I eventually came to contact Gerald

Gardner, as I have described in my book, *The Rebirth of Witchcraft*.

"I did not, as some people have suggested, introduce the concept of the Goddess into present-day Witchcraft.

'The Gods of the Witches are the oldest of all: fertility and death.'

Doreen in May 1999, just before she became ill with liver cancer. She died on 1 September 1999.

One paragraph of the article begins: 'The gods of the Witches are the oldest of all—fertility and death. A coven nowadays is led by a woman officer because of a shift in emphasis toward the Life Goddess—a woman—and away from the lord of death.' This was printed, remember, before I even joined the Craft of the Wise.

"People today have no conception of how uptight and repressive society was back in the 1950s, when old Gerald first opened up the subject of Witchcraft as a surviving old religion. You could not go into a shop then and buy a pack of Tarot cards or a book on the occult, without getting curious looks and usually a denial that they stocked any such things. There were no paperback books on the occult, except such things as *Old Moore's Almanac* and popular stuff such as how to read tea leaves. Serious books on the subject were only obtainable second-hand, at high prices. There was a built-in assumption that ordinary people were not entitled to read what they liked, or to think what they liked, and still less to do what they liked. Hence books like old Gerald's *Witchcraft Today*, first published in 1954, made all the more of an impact.

Gerald Gardner published Witchcraft Today and The Meaning of Witchcraft in the 1950s and is one of the founders of modern Wicca. Doreen Valiente was one of his High Priestesses.

A traditional Witch's necklace of amber and jet beads.

"His publishers, Riders, were really sticking their necks out in publishing it, and it was, I believe, only after having the book carefully edited by the late Ross Nichols that they agreed to do so. Even such established writers as Dione Fortune came up against this barrier of prejudice. She had to publish her most famous work of fiction, *The Sea Priestess*, herself, because no publisher in her day would touch it on account of its references to moon magic and witchery.

"Gerald was a singular character, impressive in appearance, with his wild white hair and sun-tanned face, tattoos on his arms and a big bronze bracelet on one wrist. However, he was a very kindly man, not bombastic as some would-be leaders of the occult world, but full of real out of the way knowledge and experience, gathered from many far-off places and meetings with people like Aleister Crowley and other actual practitioners of magic, not just people who talked about it.

"At first I did not question anything Gerald told me about what he said were the traditional teachings of the Old Religion. Eventually, however, I did begin to question, and to ask how much was really traditional and how much was simply Gerald's prejudices. For instance, he was very much against people of the same sex working together, especially if they were gay. In fact, he went so far as to describe gay people as being 'cursed by the Goddess.' Well, I see no good reason to believe this. In every period of history, in every country in the world, there have been gay people, both men and women. So why shouldn't mother nature have known what she was doing, when she made people this way? I don't agree with this prejudice against gay people, either inside the Craft of the Wise or outside it.

"Another teaching of Gerald's which I have come to question is the belief known popularly as 'The Law of Three.' This tells us that whatever you send out in Witchcraft, you get back threefold, for good or ill. Well, I don't believe it! Why on earth should we assume that there is a special Law of Karma, which applies only to Witches? For the Goddess' sake, do we really kid ourselves that we are that important? Yet, so I am told, many people, especially in United States, take this as an article of faith. I have never seen it in any of the old books of magic, and I think Gerald invented it.

"I am not trying to do an axe-job on old Gerald. We have had enough people doing that, usually those who would never have heard of Witchcraft if it hadn't been for him. But eventually, I also came to question how he could most solemnly swear his initiates to secrecy and then go and give an interview to some newspaper which he knew specialized in the crudest forms

of publicity. When at last I ceased working with Gerald and took up with Robert Cochrane, who claimed to be an hereditary Witch, Robert told me that the traditional Witches he knew were outraged by Gerald's activities.

"However, as I see it, nothing can stand still. We cannot live in the past. We have to look to the future. And yet, some people seem to be rather shocked to find that Witches and Pagans nowadays have web-sites on the internet, especially in the United States. Well, the internet seems to me to be rather a magical-sounding thing—the World Wide Web! Do they

Doreen with Ron Cooke, her second husband and magical partner. Doreen initiated Ron and they practiced the Craft together until his death in 1997. They joke about the stocks, once used to punish Witches.

know that one of the forms of the Goddess was a spider sitting in her great silver web? Do they know that certain voodoo cults in America refer to her as 'the Spider Queen of Space?'

"I wonder how the late Robert Cochrane would have reacted to these modern developments. He was the

The feast for Ron after he died. Doreen went to a sacred site, the Long Man of Wilmington, where she feasted with a few friends. Here Sally Griffyn and Jan Arnold sit around the altar where Doreen said her goodbyes to the love of her life and magical partner.

Magister, or male leader of a coven, whom I contacted back in the 1960s, after I had ceased to work with Gerald Gardner. He claimed to be an hereditary witch, and detested those whom he called 'the Gardnerians.' In fact, I believe he invented this word 'Gardnerian'—originally as a term of

abuse! His form of working was very different from that of Gerald Gardner. Firstly, he rejected the idea that it was necessary to work in the nude. Hence, his kind of coven has come to be known as a 'robed coven.' Its members wear robes, usually black; firstly, because they prefer to work outdoors, being closer to nature; and secondly, because they argue that if the Witch power cannot penetrate through a layer of clothing, then it must be very feeble power indeed. The black robe represents night and secrecy, and is of use as camouflage at night, when its wearers want to be able to melt into the shadows and not be seen.

"Cochrane's way of working used much less words than that of Gerald Gardner. Much of it was meditational and performed in silence. I think myself that this was probably more in keeping with the ways of our ancestors, because the majority of people in the old days could scarcely read or write, and the ritual would have been learned by heart and passed on by word of mouth. However, Cochrane observed the same ritual occasions as those of Gerald's followers: the Full

Moon and the Four Great Sabbats of Candlemas, May Eve, Lammas and Halloween. He also observed the Equinoxes and Solstices, but gave them less prominence. Wordless ritual chanting was a favorite means of raising power, as was circle dancing, often round a bonfire or symbols of the God

> **Wordless ritual chanting was a favorite means of raising power, as was circle dancing.**

and the Goddess, such as the forked wand (the stang) and the cauldron.

"I have no doubt that there was much potency in this way of working, and personally I believe it to be closer to traditional Witchcraft than Gerald's way. I think the reason why Cochrane's coven eventually broke up (described in *The Rebirth of Witchcraft*), was more to do with his personality defects and personal troubles than it was with anything wrong with his magical system. I am glad therefore to be able to

say that his workings are still being carried on, both here and in the United States, though in great secrecy.

"We talk about means of raising power; but what actually is the Witch power that is raised? It appears to be some kind of borderline energy, such as various practitioners of magic and

Doreen wearing a Witches' hat and a pentacle ring. The pentacle is the symbol most associated with Witchcraft as it represents the five elements. The stang, or forked staff, represents the Horned God of nature. She also wears the bracelet that Gardner made for her when she was his High Priestess.

Avebury stone circle, the largest henge in Britain, was one of Doreen's favorite sacred sites.

the occult have talked about in many different times and places. For instance, the Kahunas of Hawaii call it 'mana,' Hindus call it 'prana.' When in the eighteenth century the followers of Mesmer began to rediscover this energy, they talked, rather confusingly, of 'animal magnetism.' In our own day, Wilhelm Reich gave us the concept of 'orgone energy,' which seems to be very similar to what Baron Von Reichenbach in the early nineteenth century called 'od' or 'odyle,' and which he claimed to see streaming from the points of quartz crystals, a concept reminiscent of the 'crystal power' we hear so much about from

New Age practitioners today. It seems evident that all these words are describing a very similar energy, and perhaps today when people's minds are more open, we may begin to study this realm of subtle energies more closely, and perhaps rediscover what really happens when Witches gather together to raise the cone of power. This is allegedly what the Witches' pointed hat represents.

"But what should we set out to do with this power, once we have raised it? What, in fact, is the fundamental purpose of the Craft of the Wise? We are told that Witchcraft is a fertility cult. In olden times, that is probably just what it was. It was concerned with the fertility of the earth through the four seasons of the year, and with the welfare of the land and its people. It was concerned with the fundamental aspects of life: birth, death and rebirth. Hence it was basically the invocation of the Life Force itself; the 'Ancient Providence' as country people in Britain used to call it.

"However, the idea of fertility is something that goes much deeper than the hope for good crops and increase of livestock, and I am sure that it always did. There is a spiritual as well as a material fertility. There is the need for people to be alive and vital and creative. Life is here to be enjoyed, not just endured. There is a wonderful passage in Aleister Crowley's famous 'channeled' writing, *The Book of The Law*:

'Remember all ye that existence is pure joy; that all the sorrows are but as shadows; they pass and are done; but there is that which remains.'

"The initiates of the ancient Pagan mysteries were taught to say: 'I am the Child of Earth and the Starry Heaven, and there is no part of me that is not

of the Gods.' If we in our own day believe this, then we will not only see it as true of ourselves, but of other people also. We will, for instance, cease to have silly bickerings between covens, because they happen to do things differently from the way we do them. This, incidentally, is the reason why I eventually parted from Robert Cochrane, because he wanted to declare a sort of holy war against the followers of Gerald Gardner, in the

Doreen with the Long Man of Wilmington in the background, a place she visited to practice magic. The Long Man is a large image of a man carved into a chalk hillside. Reputedly ancient, his actual age is uncertain, but the nearby barrow mounds suggest he dates from the Neolithic period.

name of traditional Witchcraft. This made no sense to me, because it seemed to me, and it still does, that as Witches, Pagans, or whatever we choose to call ourselves, the things which unite us are more important than the things which divide us."

THE CHARGE
OF THE GODDESS

Whenever you have need of anything, once in the month and better it be when the Moon is full, then ye shall assemble in some secret place and adore the spirit of me who am the Queen of all Witcheries.

There ye shall assemble, ye who are fain to learn all sorcery, yet have not won its deepest secrets; to these will I teach things as of yet unknown. And ye shall be free from slavery, and as a sign that ye be truly free, ye shall be naked in your rites, and ye shall dance, sing, feast, make music, and love, all in my praise.

For mine is the ecstasy of the spirit; and mine also is joy on Earth, for my law is love unto all beings.

Keep pure your highest ideal: strive ever towards it; let naught stop you or turn you aside; for mine is the secret key which opens up the door of youth, and mine is the cup of the Wine of Life, the cauldron of Cerridwen, which is the Holy Grail of Immortality.

I am the gracious Goddess who gives the gift of joy unto the heart of man; upon Earth I give the knowledge of the Spirit Eternal; and beyond death I give peace and freedom and reunion with those who have gone before; nor do I demand sacrifice, for behold, I am the Mother of all living, and my love is poured out upon the Earth.

I who am the beauty of the green Earth and the white Moon amongst the stars, and the mystery of the waters, and the desire of the heart of man, call unto thy soul, arise and come unto me.

For I am the Soul of Nature who giveth life to the universe; from me all things proceed, and unto me all things must return; and before my face beloved of Gods and men, thine inmost divine self shall be enfoldeth in the rapture of the infinite.

Let my worship be within the heart that rejoiceth; for behold, all acts of love and pleasure are my rituals, and therefore let there be beauty and strength; power and compassion; honor and humility; mirth and reverence, within you.

And thou who thinkest to seek for me, know thy seeing and yearning shall avail thee not, unless thou knowest the mystery; that if that which thou seekest, thou findest not within thee, thou wilt never find it without thee.

For behold I have been with thee at the beginning and I am that which is attained at the end of desire.

STARHAWK
POLITICAL ACTIVIST & WITCH

Starhawk is one of the most influential Wiccans in the world. She combines political action with magical knowledge and is by her own admission a Jewish feminist, environmentalist, political-activist Witch. Her commitment to political change is combined with the teachings of the Craft to make her spiritual path one that necessarily involves direct action. Her books are renowned for encouraging the use of consensus decision making and for working against authority, which she describes as "power–over" establishments.

Her recent work involved peaceful demonstrations against the World Trade Organization in Seattle, Washington, where she was jailed by the police authorities for her stance. This is not the first time she has been willing to be incarcerated for her beliefs. She has spoken out against the nuclear power industry (which conducted nuclear tests on Hopi Indian lands), violence against women, and environmental damage caused by big business. An academic, her books are recognized as some of the most informative on Wicca and she is the founder of Reclaiming Collective, a mother coven that trains many initiates. After her activities in Seattle, in an open letter to Pagans she said:

"We worked magic in jail. We sang songs, told stories, shared meditations and learned to ground and call on the elements. About fifty of us held an impromptu ritual while waiting in a holding cell for arraignment and later danced the spiral dance. We practiced 'the art of changing consciousness at will'—and it worked. The guards, the threats, the violence and the concrete could not keep out the love, commitment, and true joy we shared."

Invocation to the Dewy One:
All-dewy Sky-sailing Pregnant Moon
Who shines for all,
Who flows through all.
Light of the world which is yourself.
Maiden, Mother, Crone,
The Weaver The Green One
Isis Astarte Ishtar
Aradia Diana Cybele
Kore Ceridwen Levanah
Luna Mari Anna
Rhiannaon Selena Demeter Mah
See with our eyes, Hear with our ears,
Touch with our hands, Breathe with our nostrils,
Kiss with our lips, Open our hearts,
Come into us!
Touch us, Change us, Make us whole.

Starhawk is renowned for ritual, and considers rites of passage an important missing link in Western culture.

"A rite of passage is a ritual that marks an important transition. If you don't mark transitions in some way, then it is like saying it's not important. For women, that's happened to us around our menstruation: nothing marks it. It is a tremendously important change in a woman's life but there's no marker for it in the larger culture. When we do ritual around it, it is a powerful act of healing for both the older women and the younger women, because it says this change in a woman's body is an important milestone which should be celebrated.

A rite of passage is a kind of symbolic cleansing or letting go of the state you have been in. It represents your entrance into a new state. You usually make an offering, fulfill a challenge, make a symbol of commitment, and receive a gift. This is followed by a little celebrating!

"A rite of passage is not just for the person going through it but for the community. A funeral is not just for the person who dies but for the

By the age of seven Shamal was already being included in family open rituals. Starhawk believes it is important that children are raised in the spiritual tradition of their parents.

people who are left behind—we get community recognition. I do think it is possible to have a rite of passage for yourself, a personal rite, but it has more impact and power if there is some way the community recognizes it as well. People do self-dedications or self-initiations. I think that kind of rite of passage is something you do to acknowledge a transition that you've made but I think there is a whole other energy and process that comes into it when you say 'and I want my community to acknowledge this.'

Shamal aged thirteen meditates on a red feather, a symbol she has chosen, at the start of a rite to celebrate her menarche.

"We do lots of rites of passage for our children. Wicca has evolved in a somewhat different way in the United States from Britain. We are not so focused on having to be initiated in order to go to the rituals. Our rituals tend either to be open to everybody, or they are private and are something

The Goddess Conference in Glastonbury in 1999, the year the Crone aspect of the Goddess was honored. Women and men come from all over the world to celebrate the Goddess.

your coven does for itself that is not open to outsiders but that is not necessarily divided between someone who is initiated and someone who is not. In Reclaiming there is an interesting and slightly conflicted view of initiation: on the one hand most of us have been through it and found it a very powerful and very important rite of passage, and on the other hand we are a consensus-based, non-authoritarian, egalitarian, non-hierarchical tradition that doesn't like the elitism

of some people being in and some people being out, and some having it and some not having it. Initiation becomes a personal process between you and the Goddess and your initiators rather than a mark of your ability to attend ritual or do magic. Some people take a philosophical position

We feel it is important for children to be raised in the spiritual tradition of their parents.

that they won't take initiation because they don't like the dividing line between ins and outs.

We feel it is important for children to be raised in the spiritual tradition of their parents—not to do it in a way that is inflicting something on them but rather encouraging them in their own spiritual, moral, and emotional growth. I co-wrote *Circle Round: Raising Children in Goddess Traditions* with Anne Hill and Diane Baker. It includes rites of passage that they have done with their own children, from baby-naming ceremonies to a ceremony that Anne did for her son when he was about five to celebrate his growth. It includes rites of passage around puberty for girls and for boys—first-blood ceremonies for our women children in our communities and rituals for the young men. The transition point for the young men is more intuitive—somewhere around the age of twelve or thirteen.

"We take girls down to the beach or to a park with their mother and we tie their hands together with a red cord and then they run together as far as the mother can run and then when she gets tired we cut them apart and let the daughter run on alone. Part of the ritual usually involves a bath or a hot tub. Or we may do it on the land in a beautiful stream or running living water. We tell the stories of our own first blood and all the secret things about menstruation and being a woman and give her the chance to ask her questions about our lives and our sexuality. Then we give her gifts and there's a celebration where she is welcomed back into the community with

both women and men—it is usually a party, feast, or a meal. It's hard because the kids from the Pagan community come but a lot of the kids don't want to tell their friends at school because it is very embarrassing and very different for them.

"For the young boys we do something similar: we tie them to the mom and then we cut them apart. The boys often do some men's stuff with the father. They don't tell us what exactly! The men did a hiking trip with one of

Starhawk in Vancouver in 2001. She was giving a series of workshops on magical activism.

the boys into the wilderness and then they were welcomed back into the community by the women. I think it is important for young boys, especially those who grow up in very female-oriented communities, for women to affirm their maleness and their sexuality. Maleness doesn't have to be seen as dangerous or violent—it can be celebrated and honored.

"We did a rite for one of the boys where his mother created a book and each of us wrote stories about times with him or contributed pictures. She made a puzzle of one picture of him and he had to take it apart and put it together. Then all the women got together with him in the center of a circle and said 'you are a man who we

love and we trust—may we always be able to say this to you.'

"I think it is important to mark menopause, to make that passage not just a physical transition or a physical loss but to celebrate it as an entry into a different state—there are gifts that come with it. Often your kids are grown (in my case it is my step kids because I never had kids of my own) but your parents are dead, you're free—that's part of the aspect of cronehood. I'm not quite there, yet I definitely feel myself moving more and more into that stage. We have done a number of menopausal rituals at Witch camp, where there is a sense of community. I've also done others for women where it has involved them

stepping into the circle of crones and younger women asking them for advice and wisdom.

"For me there is sort of a stage in-between youth and cronedom that I think of as eldership. You start to shift your focus from learning how to do something and do it well, to passing it on to the people who are coming after you. I think that's a long stage; I feel I have been in it for a quite a while. It is not linked necessarily to menopause but menopause and cronehood evolves out of that eldership. And I used to think that cronehood was that nice stage where you could kick back and have fewer responsibilities, when you could meditate on your inner wisdom. But in my case as I get closer to

cronedom, I suddenly seem to be out there on the front lines again with youth, partly because I have the free-dom to do it. There are times in your life when you really have the freedom to take risks—they are either when you are young, or when your parents are dead and the kids have left home.

"With rites of passage for death we need look at two different aspects. The first is from the perspective of the person who is dying and the second is from the perspective of those who are left behind. For the person who is dying it's a stage leading up to death: the preparation, the inner work that you undergo, to finish what you need to finish, and to mourn for what you haven't experienced, accomplished, or achieved. It's also very important and a sacred blessed act to midwife someone through that dying process, to be there when they are going through that literal passage. I was able to be there for my mother and a couple of other people in my life because, I guess, I am a Witch.

"I believe that we come back again, that each life is a learning and we come in with certain work. How you leave life is important for where that spirit is going to evolve to. Death doesn't have to be terrifying—you can go through it with support, though ultimately you go through it alone. There are a lot of different rituals or specific things that you can do, but what is most important is that sense of being connected to people who really love you and care about you as you go through that passage.

"People who die suddenly don't have that option, but we can support them by our rituals afterwards, by sending energy to that spirit, by our connection to that spirit after they are gone. In a sense there is a community

Shamal has created an altar of menstruation. Important symbols represent her coming of maturity and the letting go of childhood. There are also symbols of balance and the elements, air, fire, water, and earth.

recognition. In Reclaiming we have a huge Samhain ritual every fall with about two thousand people during which we read the names of the people who have died during that year. We set up an altar—we have lots of altars—where people can write the names of their dead. They can do a walking meditation while the names of the dead are read, or light candles.

"For the people who are left behind it is very important to mark the passing, to acknowledge the life of that person who has gone and to really

> ### We do acknowledge death, we don't shy away from it—we do talk about it.

allow yourself the time to go through the grieving process. Judy Foster was a Witch in our community who was deeply loved. She was dying of liver cancer for a number of years and in a sense we did a funeral for her before she died. There was a gathering where

people came and honored her. She read her poetry and people read poetry and spoke about what she had meant to them so that she could hear that while she was still alive.

"In the Pagan tradition we do acknowledge death, we don't shy away from it—we do talk about it, we don't have to pretend that it's not happening. I think being able to speak about it is a gift for someone who is dying. One of our friends was a young man called Raven who died of Aids. He had a problematic relationship with the community because he was a really heavy drug user and it caused a lot of problems, but when he was dying the community really came together. We moved him into a hospice and people

Women gathering at Glastonbury Tor for the 1999 solar eclipse in England. This Pagan event was attended by Witches and harkened the coming of the new millennium.

spent time with him. When he was dying there were about ten people with him through the whole process. His father, who was not at all Pagan, came for a bit. He said 'thank you for being with my son because I can't be here—it's too painful—his mother can't even come.' If we weren't there he would have died alone.

"How many men and women are dying alone because we don't have the cultural support and people don't know that it's important for them to be there for the person who is dying—to face the process and to have enough support for their grief? I felt lucky to with my mother when she was dying. She was not a spiritual person but when she was dying she opened up in surprising ways.

"Carol Crist wrote a beautiful piece about her mother's dying. She realized she was surrounded and supported by a great force of love in the universe, and that has been her conception of the Goddess ever since: I think when someone dies, the gates open and that can shine through more clearly than it does sometimes in our everyday life.

Starhawk has been an activist for much of her life and combines her spiritual and political paths.

"For many people direct action—civil disobedience, getting arrested, going to jail—can be a rite of passage. Political work has moved from being an important part of my life to being the thing that I'm doing. I thought I had a nice kind of balance between my magical work and my writing and wandering around in the woods and gardening and doing important political work.

"Now there is that sense of urgency and intensity around the environment and global trade treaties. And for the first time in years there is a movement to work with. There is an upsurge of activism and an incredible new generation who want to take action. When I was in jail with these women, I

> The Goddess in our tradition is about learning, not punishment.

realized there was a whole history and set of skills that wouldn't get passed on if people like me didn't get into the movement. Also, being able to come into activism with magical skills, tools of changing consciousness that I have learned over 20–30 years, adds a whole dimension that wasn't going to spring up without teaching it and sharing it. I decided that my work was going to center on the actions and the organizing. I haven't abandoned Witchcraft and the magic teachings, but the politics has taken center stage.

"I have spent many years teaching Witchcraft and building community, and those groups run quite well without me and in some sense it is good for them for me to pull back. It takes the focus off me as a personality and people see it's not about one person or my books or my writing. It's about something much bigger than that. It's about each person's empowerment to be priestess and a teacher and to be their own spiritual guide.

"The Goddess in our tradition is not about punishment, it's about learning. If you don't learn the lesson, she presents you with the same lesson over and over again. Over time you develop the inner skills to cope with stressful situations. I have learned a lot about dealing with community and relationships, and I don't have the excess energy or time to spend fuming about something someone said to me—I just deal with it or forget it."

Starhawk with Pat Hogan, who organized the magical activism workshops in Vancouver in 2001. Starhawk uses her drum in ceremonies and rituals.

JANET FARRAR & GAVIN BONE
WICCA IN IRELAND

Janet Farrar and Gavin Bone live in the countryside north of Dublin in Southern Ireland, in a landscape rich in ancient sacred sites. The ancient lore that speaks of Witches and Pagans surrounds them.

Janet Farrar and Gavin Bone live in the countryside north of Dublin in Southern Ireland, in a landscape rich in ancient sacred sites. The ancient lore that speaks of Witches and Pagans surrounds them. They are within an hour of Newgrange, the most spectacular Neolithic chambered tomb; the hill of Tara, the key to Eire's mythology; and their favorite, Lough Crew, which is an outstanding example of a sacred hill with chambered tomb on top. The tomb is illustrated inside with marvellous ancient carvings.

Janet was initiated by Alex and Maxine Sanders in London in 1970. She was married to Stewart Farrar until his death in 2000. Together they wrote several seminal books, including *The Witches' Bible Compleat.* In this they describe the seasonal festivals, rituals, and spiritual path of Wiccans. Later the two authors published a book together with Gavin Bone called *The Healing Craft,* which discusses Wiccan healing techniques. In 1976 Janet and Stewart moved to Ireland and set up their first coven there. After researching *Eight Sabbats for Witches,* they developed their own style of Wicca. Janet is something of a "celebrity Witch," which she speaks out against in this interview, but her charm, wit, and intelligence make her a striking speaker on the Craft.

Gavin is known to champion Witches who do not come from a specific lineage and he speaks about his belief in the power of self-dedication to the Craft. Janet and Gavin were recently handfasted in a traditional Wiccan wedding in which the hands are symbolically tied together as a symbol of love. They now live in Eire, writing and looking after stray cats.

Janet: "We call ourselves Wiccan, but we do not label ourselves any specific tradition, regardless of our roots. This does confuse some Wiccans—if you really need to label us, call us 'Progressive Wiccan' but remember

A Pagan placing flowers in a sacred well in County Clare, Ireland. Offerings have been left in this ancient well since pre-Christian times.

that the first rule of this tradition is that there is no such thing as tradition as we all follow our own path. We consider all spirituality, particularly Paganism, to be organic in nature and therefore a growth process. Hence, our way of practicing Wicca is very different to how we first practiced it, or how we practiced it when we wrote our books. We obey the natural law that if something doesn't evolve it becomes extinct—this applies as much to spiritual practices as it does to species! We do not denigrate any other

method of Wiccan practice—it is just no longer correct for us. In Ireland social and environmental factors have required us to develop in a different way to the US or Europe.

"We no longer use the degree system as first taught to us, but have developed it into a more natural system based on the idea that 1st equals Dedication, 2nd equals Initiation and 3rd equals Eldership. We still use the terms 1st, 2nd, and 3rd to prevent confusion. We guide students, but don't 'teach' them as if they were pupils in a secondary school. We act as mentors for those who want learn Wicca, realizing that everyone has their own individual path. We still expect our students to know the basics but encourage them to specialize in an occult or healing field.

"We consider Wicca to be like being 'under Holy Orders' within Paganism, just as there are Dominican Priests and so on in Catholicism—Wicca is *a* Priest/esshood, but not *the* Priest/esshood of Paganism. Recently, we have become more and more convinced that the origins of Wicca are in the healing arts, with magical practice being a part of this (hence the publication of our latest book *The Healing Craft: Healing Practices for Witches and Pagans*).

"Over the years we have come to realize that the central core of Wicca has to be connection with deity. This, after all, is what makes it a priesthood: connection with and service to an individual Goddess/God. All Wiccan training should really center around this concept. Wicca has been moving slowly towards this since Gerald Gardner first came out of the broom closet in 1951.

"Evolution is an important word to explain the development of Wicca. A Pagan Priesthood must above all else obey the laws of nature, the laws of the Goddess.

"What started as one way of doing things with the writings of Gerald Gardner and Doreen Valiente in *The Book of Shadows* has spread into a myriad of traditions and diverse forms. This is evolution at work. Nature loves diversity, as it encourages survival.

"If we look at the many different traditions of Wicca that exist today we

A dolmen or ancient burial site, part of the sacred landscape of Ireland.

can see that they have adapted to their social surroundings. This can even be brought down to the level of the coven, where we see even these individual magical groups adapting differently. A hive-off coven will always be a quite different entity to its parent group. Of course this has occasionally not happened, particularly in Wiccan traditions where they have kept to a dogmatic system of laws. Inevitably, in the end these groups have either adapted or gone the way of the dinosaurs.

Janet Farrar, Stewart Farrar and Gavin Bone in 1999. Stewart was very elderly and he died soon after this photograph was taken.

"This is why we have seen the fall of the major religious institutions in recent years: failure to adapt quickly to society's needs. Because Paganism is evolving it is filling this gap, just as foliage fills the gap in a forest where a tree has fallen. It is why Paganism is drawing so many young people at present, as can be seen by the media's interest in it in television and film. It is destined to become a major force in the religious world by the end of the twenty-first century. Wicca has played the most important part of this growth process within the neo-Pagan revival. When you look back, it is obvious that Wicca's purpose has been to launch the neo-Pagan movement and encourage its growth.

"Being a Priest/Priestess must be about service to God/Goddess, and it must include a certain level of humility, although this is service, not slavery—a symbiotic relationship between the material and spiritual worlds where neither one overrides

> **We have felt guided in what we do ... and our life has begun to revolve around service to that deity.**

the other. Gavin is a healer, while Janet is a counsellor; when you look at all the magical traditions it becomes obvious that they all originate in healing traditions carried out in the shamanistic practices of our ancestors. As Priest and Priestess we seek to continue this tradition.

"As far as we are concerned it was the connection with our deity, Freya, that was our true initiation. At different times, both of us had what could be best referred to as an epiphany. The experience was such that we now understand the Christian Evangelical experience referred to as being 'born again'; the main difference was that we understood the mechanics of what was happening. Ever since that time we have felt guided in what we do as Priest and Priestess, and our life has begun to revolve around service to that deity.

"Wicca is a mystery tradition, as all ancient priesthoods were. We have learnt that it is impossible to give away the true secrets of Wicca as they are experiential.

"*A Witches' Bible* is the combination of two books together: *Eight Sabbaths for Witches* and *The Witches' Way*. The publisher chose the title—I can't stand it. Neither of us saw writing as a mission. Stuart had been a writer all his life, in fact he has done everything except stage plays. When he was commissioned to write *What Witches Do*, his first book, by Alex and Maxine

A Pagan wishes at the Hag's Chair while Gavin Bone watches (background left). The Hag's Chair is on Lough Crew near to Gavin and Janet's home in County Meath in Southern Ireland. It is reputed to be an ancient wishing stone associated with Witches.

Aleister Crowley's chalice, now in the Museum of Witchcraft. Crowley was a magician who was once initiated as a Witch but gained an infamous reputation as a ritualist.

A standing stone in Ireland. Janet and Gavin consider it important to connect with the local deities and spirits of the land.

Sanders, he found the philosophy and the spirituality he had searched for all his life. He carried on writing about the Craft because he loved it so much. He knew that there was more to it than the knowledge that he gained from the Sanders and from those original *Books of Shadows*. He wanted to put meat on the bones. I did a lot of the research for him. I ploughed my way through Ireland, through every library, through every country village, asking as many questions as I could, gathering information from everywhere. It wasn't until 1991, when we

came over here to the United States, that we realized just how the religion had started to spread—we had been out of contact with Britain for six or seven years. America was a whole new experience, a new doorway. We'd read people like Starhawk, for example, but what we saw growing here had outstripped Europe—here was a thriving community who were beginning to find their own spirituality through this whole philosophy. It was not something I had gone out of my way to do and certainly I've got no regrets, but if I could turn the hands of the clock back, I'm not sure I would want to write those books again.

"I'm in a rather unusual situation and it's mainly because of Stuart. He was always the perfect gentleman, and when we came here we suddenly found ourselves being treated like stars and I couldn't handle that. I turned myself into the clown of the Craft, simply because I didn't like the total adoration that we had thrust upon us and the only way to climb off that pedestal was to act the idiot. So I've had to become a sacred clown. I'm the jester. But then I discovered there's

need lineage because it gives them a sense of legitimacy."

Gavin: "If you've had a spiritual experience, you don't need that legitimacy because it's coming from within you. It's coming from the self. They're still caught up in this cult-figure mentality which occurred in Wicca with names like Gardner, Sanders, and Starhawk. Deriving your

Nobody quite knows where I'm going to pop up next and what bubble I'm going to burst.

power from a figure. The problem is when people see their initiation as being from a person, not from spirit."

Janet: "Another problem arises through us writing books like *Eight Sabbats*: we get e-mails from Japan and they are worshipping Cernunnos and Aradia. These don't belong in Japan. Again, they are not connecting with deity directly. In our practice in Ireland, we have our own personal deities.

something very useful about being the joker in the pack. It means that we can now travel not just in the United States but back in Britain and to places like Australia. I can use that joker in the pack to stir up a cauldron, and that cauldron has been stagnant for a long time. I find it's a good way of doing it because nobody quite knows where I'm going to pop up next and what bubble I'm going to burst. The bubbles are dogma, the lack of spirituality, and lineage—the idea that 'only a witch can make a witch.' Stuart thought it was rubbish. So did Doreen Valiente. And many people who were the founders considered it irrelevant. It's the followers today that

"These personal deities are genetic. They're the ancestral deities. On top of that, Gavin and I share the same ancestral deity. One of her aspects is that she is a cat goddess. She expects every cat in the neighborhood to be looked after in our house, which means I open the window and another stray walks in. I've had to set up a shrine to Bast, the Egyptian cat Goddess, and Bast has her own coven of cats on her altar where I keep a candle burning for them. So even the cats have their own ancestral deity in the house, but because we are living in Ireland, when we do rituals there we also address the genus loci. For us, in our case, it's a little-known deity called Tlachta, an ancient goddess of witchcraft who's older than the legends of the Danaeans. She doesn't work outside County Meath: that's her one particular place. So our house sits on Tlachta's lap. Now we have no problem with her and our ancestral deity because the place where our house stands was Viking—Norse territory— and as our ancestral deity is of Saxon/Norse origin, the two girls get on fine. And all three of them have connections with cats. So we have Tlachta, the ancestral deity, and Bast all happily co-existing side by side. And a house full of strays!

"That's the goddess principle. For the god principle, again locally, we have a horned deity. Nobody knows what his name would have been but there are strong indications that he is linked to the Irish god Lugh, who has a connection with the stag. Many of

Janet Farrar has been an important influence on modern Wicca.

his legends are the legends of St Patrick—or rather St Patrick's are Lugh's legends. So Lugh is happily hanging around with us. Another ancestral deity for both Gavin and myself is Norse and he has a connection with animals as well."

Gavin: "We got manifestations of Aesculapius when we were writing *The Healing Craft* because the manuscript attracted his attention. I reclaimed the Hippocratic oath as a Pagan ritual. Of course, Aesculapius is very strong, because doctors around the world still take the Hippocratic oath and when they do they invoke Aesculapius, which keeps him active. He's in our culture still. So we got a little statue of Aesculapius.

"In Greek he's called Asklepios. That's much easier than the Latin. Other deities pop up and we have experiences with them but they're just one-off little experiences."

Janet: "In a sense, I tend to see myself as a sort of divine DNA, for want of a better word. A Christian example would be Jesus as the healer, not as the human but as the created god figure. Jesus, Aesculapius, and

Apollo are all healing deities. You can see all of them as the same basic DNA of the healing principle of creation or of spirituality or, for want of a better word, godhead, and then put them in the countries of their origin. Their DNA will take on the pattern or flavor of the country of origin. It's like having strawberry, vanilla, and raspberry: they're all lovely, they're all tasty, they're all good to eat, and they're all fruit. That's the way I tend to see it.

"I see science and mathematics as the robe of the god. Watching somebody who is a great mathematician or

A sacred well dedicated to the cure of toothache, in the Burren, County Clare. Paganism is thriving in Ireland, and little offerings can be seen around the well.

a great physicist is absolute magic—the excitement, the childlike ecstasy on their face when they are working with a problem. They are dealing directly with the lineological aspect of creation and they are pulling the god through themselves in the sheer wonder of what they're discovering."

Megalithic art inside Lough Crew chambered tomb.

Gavin: "There isn't a dichotomy in this. With Christianity there was a dichotomy in the Middle Ages: you couldn't be scientific and a Christian until the Renaissance, but in ancient times Paganism and science went hand in hand. Christianity destroyed science for over a millennium."

Janet: "With quantum physics scientists go so far with theory that it has to become metaphysical, and then suddenly it becomes spiritual. You can't escape it at that level.

"Some of the greatest minds in the scientific world today have that divine, childlike quality. Stephen Hawkins is a classic example."

Gavin: "Monotheistic culture compartmentalizes. It divides into boxes such as natural and supernatural, science and religion. Even Christianity

To be a Priest or Priestess you must experience spirit. You become a servant of spirit.

is divided into different sects of Protestant and Catholic. They even regard religion and spirituality as two different things and if we're not careful we'll do the same. But when you start to move East, you find those divisions don't exist. For instance, in India you find fusions between Hinduism and Buddhism. In Japan, you'll find a Shinto-Buddhist temple—there's a fusion of two different spiritual values. In Western culture you find division and unfortunately in

Paganism and Wicca, we've started to do the same thing because of monotheistic influences. We're putting things in boxes and causing divisions.

A witch is principally a Priest or Priestess who serves spirit. To be a

Janet: "That's where my problem comes from trying to analyze what is a witch, because what Gavin has just said applies to the priesthoods of other faiths as well. A friend of ours went to a Hindu temple because he

Priest or Priestess you must experience spirit. You become a servant of spirit and to that end you ultimately serve spirit by serving mankind and serving nature. That is how I perceive it. With that comes many responsibilities but what is at the core of being a priest or priestess is this connection with deity: at the end of the day it has to be experiential."

couldn't find any witches in his area and after a week, one of the priests said, 'I'm not being rude but you're the only white face in our temple—are you a Hindu?' And the lad said, 'No, I'm a Wiccan.' The priest asked what a Wiccan was and our friend told him. The priest said, 'You're a Hindu then.' Now you see my problem —what is a witch? How do you put a label on it?"

Diane Darling, an American Wiccan Priestess, meditates on the Hag's Chair at Lough Crew.

LIBATION TO BRID AT THE SACRED WELL

This spell shows the magical work we now use and our connection to the land that we live in and its culture. We have moved away from Kabbalistic-based ceremonial ritual magic and are more "deity oriented" in our work. We put all our magical requests through the myriad of faces that are the God and Goddess, in this case Bríd.

THE RITUAL

At sunrise, carry three stones and some pebbles to a sacred well, and place them to the east of the water. Kneeling before the well, clear away any debris that has fallen into the water and say:

"Holy Bríd, bright threefold Lady, as I clean this well I ask for myself to be cleansed that I may be a pure vessel to heal those who have need of thee."

Anoint your forehead, your throat, and heart with water from the well. Pick up your largest stone and walk clockwise around the well saying:

"Great Bríd, mistress of healing, I dedicate this pure water to your honor so that all those who would seek health and hope might gain their desires through your gentle touch."

Place your first stone in its permanent position. Taking the second largest stone, repeat the process, this time saying:

"Mighty Queen, divine inspirer, fill me with your knowledge. By gazing deep into your watery depths may I become filled with the inspiration required to make me a fitting vessel for your work."

Kneel before the well and contemplate its depths. Place the second stone in position. Take up the final stone, walk around the well, and say:

"Lady of the Artisans and Craftsmen, I ask for your blessing upon my endeavors. Let this healing well bring color and joy to weary hearts; sweet smells and peace of mind to saddened souls, hope and renewed vigor to enfeebled bodies. Inspire me to plant strong herbs for healing, and colorful flowers for your delight here, in your honor."

Place your final stone in its place (the stones now form a triangle). Rinse the pebbles in the well, visualizing each one as a molecule of Bríd's healing power, and place them in the triangle. Return to the well, bow three times and say:

"Spirit of this well, I ask you in Bríd's name to watch and guard this water for our Lady. For this service I thank you."

Decorate a nearby tree with rags and ribbon, and thank the guardian for its protection. Thank Bríd for her aid in whatever way your heart tells you to, for her inspiration has now begun!

EDMUND
HIGH PRIEST & WRITER

Edmund is the pseudonym for a High Priest who has decided to remain anonymous in order to protect his regular work. He is an expert in the history of Paganism and Witchcraft and he gives lectures, papers, and broadcasts on these subjects, and on many other subjects as well. A widely published professional author, he is well regarded in his field. Always ferociously researched and cool headed, he breaks new ground as he reveals what truly are the rites of Pagans and which ceremonies have been borrowed from other sources. In this quest he strives to represent authentically Wiccans, who are reliant on often misleading images.

Edmund first encountered Wicca in his teens, during the late 1960s, and has been a practicing Pagan ever since. However, he only became widely known to witches in general during the 1990s. This was partly because it was only from the late 1980s that national networks such as the Pagan Federation developed in Britain which could introduce witches to each other, and partly because he only then felt sufficiently well-established in his career to risk the possible problems of being identified as a Wiccan.

He has worked as a High Priest for a decade now, and during this time he has suppported nine different High Priestesses. He worked with some of the High Priestesses for several years; some he worked with only for the short period during which they had no suitable man to fulfill the role in their own covens. During this time he has initiated many people into various covens and has become established in the role of an elder in his regional network of Wiccan groups.

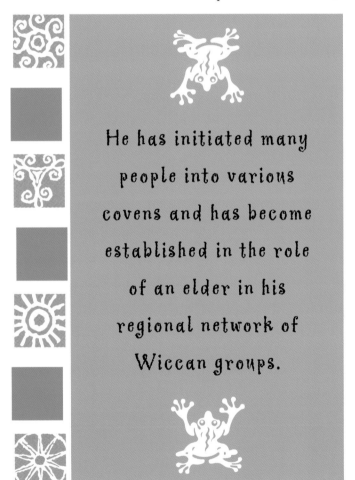

He has initiated many people into various covens and has become established in the role of an elder in his regional network of Wiccan groups.

"I have chosen to write under a pseudonym because I realize that as I am a writer for a living and relatively well-known in the media, my value as a speaker on Paganism and as a mediator has been very firmly established. When the caring services, the police, the academics, and the people on the

Jack in the Green, a May Day God figure whose maypole refers to his potent sexuality.

The Green Man at a May Day festival in the Welsh Borders. It is considered lucky to kiss him on this day.

outside want to know objective data about Witches, they turn to me. And although they recognize I can't possibly know about all this stuff unless I practice it, the fiction is still needed that I am in some way objective. People who are in trouble as Witches, whose neighbors are being nasty to them, find it useful when someone like me, who has a fairly public position, is brought in to mediate and to

explain that things are alright. I have studied the background of the Pagan/Witchcraft movement and can set them right on the facts. I am one of the few people who, because of my books, occupies this middle ground.

"It is hard to get men to talk about their experiences of working in the Craft. I am quite troubled by some

From the beginning Wicca was built around the concept of female power.

some of the opinions of the historian, Ronald Hutton, but one thing he says is spot on. He says that the special qualities needed for the role of the High Priest combine those of the poet, the teacher, the parent, the cleric, the actor, the orator, and the medium. It is one of the toughest jobs out.

"In the 1950s men played a much more significant role in Wicca, but in theory women were predominant from the start. The very first text of Wicca,

Witchcraft Today (1954) by Gerald Gardner, says that a man alone cannot run a coven. If she has to, a woman can strap on a sword and take on the role of High Priest. A man can't take the role of High Priestess.

From the beginning Wicca was built around the concept of female power and I think that a lot of men have no trouble with that in principle but in practice it is rather hard to handle—always having to be a podium for somebody else. The only way I find that easy is to decentralize the power: I regard myself as being in service to the entire coven and I am a podium for everybody in it, helping draw out the best of them.

"There is an equality ascribed to men and women in the Craft. If the stronger personality happens to be the High Priest, then often he will be dominant in practice, but in theory although everyone is equal, there is a margin of leadership for the female. Because this is so essential to Wicca's self-image and its history, I am very happy to support it. If Wicca depends upon being a countercultural religion to honor things which have been

A Wiccan Priest meditating on the pentacle, symbol of the element earth.

feared or derided in mainstream Western society in the last one thousand years then I think it is important to keep that tradition going.

"I don't think that the post feminist condition is going to make a big difference to the role of men in Wicca and there are so few places left in society in which women can expect some natural margin of leadership that to preserve it in Wicca seems absolutely essential. I think that as a man I found adapting to that situation one of my greatest challenges and one of my greatest pleasures. I wouldn't regard myself as being a well-rounded man if I didn't have this capacity to be a support system.

Edmund in his temple, wearing a hooded robe to conceal his identity. The altar is in the foreground

There is a long history of secrecy in the Craft. Edmund would like to be out but keeps his identity secret. The Craft is a also a mystery religion: a sacred oath is taken to preserve its secrets.

"Mystery cults require a certain sort of cavelike effect—the closed circle of the magical universe. It works much better if you have some sense of danger or alienation around you but unfortunately I found that the danger is very real: at certain points in my life when I lived more openly I had to put up with derision and disrespect from colleagues, pupils, and friends, although I never suffered anything that resembled systematic persecution. As soon as people see me again as an objective expert who writes about Wicca but isn't personally involved, the balance is restored and everybody is happy. So I have been pushed into preserving secrecy but, left to my own devices, I would live openly as a witch.

A renowned historian, Edmund has much to contribute to a history of Wicca.

"There are two histories of Wicca: one of them we can recover, the other is much more debatable and may be lost. We can situate it in our cultural history of the British Isles in the last 200 years. You can see some themes very clearly: a reverence for a goddess, the night sky, and the natural world; a huge new interest in the horned god of nature; a desire for an ethic of self-expression and reunion within your own imagination with the natural world; and a desire to have a celebration of human sexuality. These things developed since the romantic movement a couple of hundred years ago. Wicca represents an extreme distillation of them, and combines them into a very potent modern religion. So that's the history we can recover.

"The history which is perhaps more important to Wiccans is probably lost: it is how Wicca developed specifically. All we can say for sure is that it was revealed to the world by a retired colonial civil servant called Gerald Gardner. There are two big questions there that may never be solved. Firstly, was there a big Wicca movement around before Gardner

Houses similar to Edmund's. Like many Wiccans, Edmund's temple is in his house.

from which he just took the structure we know today? This is insoluble because it is in the best interests of non-Wiccan Witches to say that they're as old or older than Wicca, and as yet there is no hard evidence either way. The problem of whether Gardner himself made it all up is probably insoluble at this stage because Gardner didn't write much himself, he shared the writing. We have only the haziest idea of his

Alex Sander's God mask. In the 1960s Alex was responsible for the revival of Wicca known as the Alexandrian line.

collaborators before the late 1940s: he could have been the moving spirit in a circle or he could have been just one of a group—we just don't know.

"In Western culture, the dominant definition of religion since the Ancient Greeks is its relationships with supernatural beings, its transactions with the divine. By that definition, Wicca scores heavily. What

Wicca does really well is to put people in a really intense and immediate relationship with the supernatural. It leaves them a very wide margin of personal interpretation of what is happening. It is very good at enabling people to work together in small, very tightly knit groups to achieve spiritual experiences of tremendous intensity. That's what it does best.

"Its countercultural framework heightens the intensity: the primacy of the feminine; the ethic which establishes that you are free to express yourself to your full potential provided that you harm nothing else, which is a really tough ethic; and the sense of a close kinship with the natural world. It is often a kind of distilled natural world, as Wiccans are perfectly happy working in a front room like mine—they don't have to go out and roll in the leaves, so it's often very abstract and all the more powerful for that. The really important thing is to create a circle about nine feet wide in which you can put a number of people and pressure cook them spiritually to produce amazing results. That's what we try to do in the covens.

"Very rarely have I encountered anything I would call an uncanny spiritual experience. I am a great rationalizer. Put me in most spiritual experiences and I'll be able to tell you exactly why I am happy with the idea that all this stuff is coming out of me

Wicca puts people in a really intense and immediate relationship with the supernatural.

and my fellow people—it's not coming from the outside, we are working with symbols. Just occasionally the effect is so strong that I will have doubts but that always happens by accident. There is something about magic that is quite capricious.

"In many ways Wicca is a classic example of a postmodern religion: it doesn't demand faith. It doesn't have scriptures. It has bodies of work in ritual which enable you to experience the divine directly in your own way. It is possible to be a romantic

agnostic and even an atheist Wiccan. You could have no literal personal belief in your deities but still work with them as symbolic forces—and they work on that level. On the other hand you also have people who not only believe in them completely but also know them as personalities in the most powerful theistic sort of religious experience.

Edmund's altar with his horned stang, a Wiccan symbol of the God.

A coven of Witches dance round a tree to raise energy during a rite. Dancing and chanting are used the world over to energize and enter trance states.

"I am also very bad at spellcraft. I have immense rationalist blocks on believing in it. I am quite good at making it work but hanged if I know why. My coven does an enormous amount of ritual to honor things and transform ourselves, to solve problems, and to alter the world around us. It relatively rarely tries to solve a specific problem. When we do that it tends to work but I'm not sure why or how.

"A Witch's working tools are symbolic, they are not like a golf club which you must have to whack a ball. They are more like a child's water wings—psychologically they help you to swim but you don't actually need them to swim. I think that magic works best when it is given something specific to do. There are really two different extremes in the spectrum of magic. One is the feel good factor: somebody is not feeling good so they ask you to do some work for them (healing) and that makes them feel better anyway. But if somebody is in a coma, or you have a child who is seriously ill and fighting for life, there's no placebo effect, and yet magic seems to work. If somebody's life is on a knife edge and traditional remedies have failed, then magic can work. It needs white-hot emotion, passion, and real direction and then it does seem to happen. I don't know why, but in these situations you are not going to worry too much about the theory.

"Magic to me is a completely opaque mysterious chain of causation by which a deeply felt will attaches to a physical result. That's straightforward operative magic. It comes into its own when you are dealing with a critical physical problem that seems to be against the flow of nature and needs a remedy. There is a different definition of magic, which I use in

other situations. It is a means of bringing about a change in the relationship to the world around you which changes things that happen in it—in other words, you change yourself and the world around you alters to fit your new self—that's the kind of thing you do all the time in Wicca.

"To become a Wiccan High Priest you really, really, really have to love women a lot and really find them fascinating. You have to enjoy working with them more or less on an equal basis and be prepared to yield for the sake of female empowerment. You also really have to be fascinated by people.

"The Wiccan theory is that covens are top downwards—in other words they gush from the loins of a well-partnered High Priestess and High Priest. That is right, but good covens are built from the bottom upwards. You have to help your trainees and slowly build up a working relationship with their talents. This constant sense of empowering others is the real magic. The more you empower the people with whom you are working, the better the group is and therefore you learn very quickly that one of the

Craft's greatest secrets it that by helping give magic to others and helping them express themselves, you get to do things that you would never be able to do alone. Wicca is a cooperative venture. And the names of High Priest and High Priestess can so often cloak the essentially cooperative way in which a coven always has to work in order to function as a person. You can be a Witch alone, it just is not the kind of Witch I am."

Witches' talismans from the Wichcraft Museum. Talismans can be empowered with energy for healing or transformation.

A Priestess invoking the Goddess during a circle. Wicca puts people in direct contact with the divine.

THE APPEAL TO THE DIVINE

For I am the power of the swelling hills and the sprouting woodland, of the gliding rivers and the restless ocean; and you who would seek me must know this—that you are a being, like myself, divine. Only in this we differ, that while I am for ever renewed, you suffer endless change.

Seek me then, not with flattery nor with servility, but with emulation; for you can never truly know divinity until you have felt it in your own muscles and your gushing veins. If you would have beauty and joy, then create them, and I shall give you more. If you would have law and justice, then provide them for others, and I shall accord them to you. Make this world more glorious, and I shall show you more worlds. I do not ask of you obedience; I require daring instead. I do not demand service; I demand heroism.

In this you will know a warning: that my way is not for the timid. For I am the lover of the Furies as well as of the Nymphs of the meadows. Call to me and I shall be with you in the storm as well as in the silence, in the shadows as well as in the sunlight, and in the battle as well as in the temple. And oh, my sister yet to be born, I shall be with you at the time when all changes end.

DAWN HARDY & TONY MEADOWS
A MAGICAL PARTNERSHIP

Dawn and Tony come from different ends of the Wiccan spectrum, yet manage to blend the different techniques and add their own recipe for successful Witchcraft. Dawn was initiated by Alex and Maxine Sanders approximately thirty years ago into an Alexandrian coven. She was reinitiated and adopted by Vivianne and Chris Crowley, who practice a mix of Gardnerian and Alexandrian Wicca. Tony was initiated by Vivianne and Chris Crowley. He met Dawn ten years ago, and they formed a coven that takes teaching from both schools. They were handfasted in a traditional Wiccan marriage.

They run a coven near the Welsh borders, in the heart of ancient sites with Pagan associations and are heavily influenced by the landscape and the seasons. Their rural lifestyle allows them to honor the land.

Dawn's shop in Shrewsbury sells Wiccan items as well as New Age paraphernalia. Originally an artist (he illustrated the Llewellyn's Witches calendar for many years), Tony is now a networking and computer software technician. They run a coven near the Welsh borders, in the heart of ancient sites with Pagan associations and are heavily influenced by the landscape and the seasons. Their rural lifestyle allows them to honor the land, and they collect sacred water from St Winifred's Well, a natural spring reputed to have healing properties.

Dawn runs Wicca study groups from her shop and offers correspondence courses for those who wish to study from afar. Dawn and Tony have an influx of potential initiates even though they are based in the country. They have an idyllic cottage with space for outdoor ritual, and in the garden they have created a secluded Witch's paradise. With temples both indoors and outdoors, their situation is enviable compared with city Wiccans, who often make do with their living rooms.

Tony: "Our coven has a mixed Alexandrian/Gardnerian background; we have a rounded balance of training of modern Craft. We have developed our work to form something suited to our locality, which is fairly remote.

The chalice and the staff. This is the symbolic Great Rite, where the phallic wand meets the womblike cup and the water within is charged with energy.

The Welsh borders has a magic all its own. We rely on deepening our relationship with the natural world rather than on formal esoteric ritual.

"When I started, the Craft had an esoteric rather than an earth focus. Ritual was very formalized because it was urban based and focused on inner work rather than being overtly related to the spirit of the place.

"From Vivianne and Chris Crowley's group in London we gained an understanding of and respect for formal training of initiates. Wicca has a structured training that works as an apprenticeship, so you have a theoretical side but also deeply embedded is a practical side where

> **You have a theoretical side but also deeply embedded is a practical side.**

things aren't explained to you but are shown. You practice until you attain an understanding and mastery. That's really where advancement and progression comes, by grasping the intangibles—grasping them in a way that is very carefully focused. It is subtle and cleverly crafted—my initiators were very wise and skillful teachers and we have attempted to train people here in a similar fashion."

Dawn: "I was initiated by Alex Sanders about thirty years ago. I entered the Craft when I was eighteen and at that time there wasn't a Pagan Federation, nor any way of being able to worship with like-minded people or to investigate ones inner promptings. There wasn't the wealth of books that there are now. I searched through Eastern books with a religious basis and I resonated with certain truths, but there was always something missing. I met an old boyfriend who was already involved in the Craft. My initial reaction was 'don't talk to me about such scary things' but when he began to talk about celebrating the Wheel of the Year and it being natively based and to do with nature—as well as magic and spell making—it became more attractive and I went to Alex and Maxine's open evenings. I resonated with the people there, although a lot of them were older than me. There was something that united us straight away. No matter how ordinary the people are, they live slightly on the edge of society, which brings the bizarre into people's lives. They were often a little between the

worlds. People were open with each other—they accepted you because you had a common searching, so you met on a deeper level than usual, although you might not click with them superficially at all. And it was fun. There was a lot of going down to the pub, and the wacky stuff like television cameras—all very exciting when you are young. There was a bit of a naughty side as well because Witchcraft had (and still has) so many connotations of dark and evil. We knew how bright it was, and other people didn't know at all.

"In those days they used to spring initiation on people. It was done on the spur of the moment and there was

Tony in the outdoor grove that the couple use for ritual. Rural Witches, they have developed a close relationship with the land.

Madron's Well (Mother's Well) in Cornwall, England, is still a center of Goddess worship. This ancient well is regularly adorned with corn dollies like the one shown in the picture and its waters are reputed have healing properties.

were initiated as well, we used to celebrate sabbats with them. Then I moved to Shropshire, where the idea was to tie in rituals with the land. Alex and Maxine focused on learned books and myth, with a lot of Kabbalistic and Egyptian work. We wanted to look less to myth, more to the mysteries of the land. Some people here were trying to live off the land and we wanted to work on the land in a more open way in a community of like-minded people. We run a training coven. It is not like it was at Alex's, where we were trained and encouraged to leave to form our own groups, thus helping modern Witchcraft to grow. We are not trying to make as many Witches as possible. There is a feeling that we are growing together, not just training.

"In order to create a coven we ran a Wicca study group. It was going to be for six months but they all stayed and we did another six months and then we initiated ten of them more or less together. We knew it would be hard work at the start, and there was an element of sibling rivalry with them all being initiated at once. It was very

a sense of fear—you had to be ready. It kept you on your toes and made you very sharp. I remained a member of the coven until I had my daughter. Then it was more difficult to go out so we celebrated by ourselves and, because other people in my family

intense and really took over our lives. Then for individual and personal reasons, people gradually left until we were down to ourselves and just one other covener. After this time of giving, we found ourselves growing with this one other person. We were

It is a journey of understanding of self, stretching of self, and a flowering of self.

able to do things for ourselves. But then that yearning to make more Witch babies came up again, as did our ingrained sense of responsibility to pass on the tradition."

Tony: "Some of the original bunch came back after taking a break. Some took the teaching into a wider community in different ways, which was good. Although not formally teaching Wicca, two have reinvigorated folk dance with a Pagan element.

"The Craft consists of an apprenticeship, and a relationship between

Dawn picks herbs from the countryside near her home for use in ritual. She prefers to use locally grown herbs whenever possible.

tradition, an individual, and the Gods. The tradition gives it a corpus of shared experience and a family connection with others, however far that stretches back. For the individual it is a journey of understanding of self, stretching of self, and a flowering of self. It's also very important to have an appreciation of the gods and an understanding of the workings of the Gods and the patterns of change that occurs within the natural world. So when people leave the group, they can invest the outer world with a fragment

The pond in Dawn and Tony's garden is a focus for outdoor water rituals. They have created a secluded garden that is a perfect setting for ceremony.

The kiss over the blessed wine: "I offer you this chalice that you may never thirst."

"Although new folk join our coven, the ones that have remained have taken a more focused priesthood. We work with a formal degree system and have a core of the higher degrees. At that point there is a focus about serving the Craft and its continuity; building the strength, breadth, and experience of the Craft; and ministering to the Gods as well as to the family, to the hearthfire, to friends and the outer world. There is an inner focus that defines the High Priest and High Priestess. The people who remain have taken that devotion, love, worship, joy, and pleasure to another level, where they focus that inwards."

Dawn "The absolute essence of the Craft is a constant awareness of the Gods. The Gods are what we feel when we feel our strengths inside. They are what we see when we see a tree buckling in the wind and recognize that essence of life, when we see the shimmering mist and we cloak it with our own imagination to form images. Or it is when we look into a flower that has come into bloom and it reaches a deep part of us and we feel a sense of worship. It's carrying that knowledge

or a pearl of that. A large number of people who come to the Craft come in a state of spiritual unfolding or awareness, where they have to break out from the life that they had before. The Craft often proves a catalyst that moves them into doing something else, usually something in the community because the Craft is geared up for service.

The couple dancing the maypole at a May day celebration. The pole represents the erect phallus and the weaving of the ribbons around it represent the female sexuality. The dance is an ancient fertility dance.

have a deeper meaning and things flow. Everything has a rhythm because we work so much with the rhythms of life and the seasons.

"We are always aware of the seasons on a deeper level because we are worshipping and reflecting the dance of the God and Goddess throughout the year. That feeds our natural rhythms and we become more in tune and understand why we're feeling reflective in autumn and excited at Imbolc. We can bring our lives into that rhythm and we know there are times when it is appropriate to make decisions about mundane matters, and times it is too difficult, when we have to allow ourselves to be really dreamy about things.

"You become in tune with life and aware of the Goddess. You know something greater than yourself, especially at times of personal stress or when you are trying to help people through stress. And you know you are much greater than yourself. How you can help a person may come to you in dreams. You know you can reach a part of a greater whole in your life and this helps you. You feed this wholeness

and awareness that you've probably been a Witch before and know that you will be again. You know that you will always be searching for these mysteries, now and then touching with something that feels so deep that you just know. Everything seems to

with meditation and ritual and at other times it feeds you. It's a constant relationship where you are giving to the Gods and they are giving to you. You petition the Gods—sometimes asking for things and sometimes giving thanks—so everything has a

> # Being in the Craft is like being part of an extended family across much of the world.

rhythm to it. Even people who don't know about your Craft sense a positive difference in your nature, even if you don't promote the Craft by talking about it much. But when people do find out about it, they respect it because they recognize that it is harmonious and whole.

"Being in the Craft is like being part of an extended family that crosses the world. You can stay with people in other countries who welcome you and with whom you share rituals. You have a meaningful and good time with them."

Wicca celebrates the sacred union of male and female, to achieve perfect balance. This can be expressed in a magical partnership beautifully.

Tony "It would be difficult to be in a relationship with Dawn if she wasn't a Witch; it's such an integral part of

Witches frequently gather together for May Day celebrations. Women often wear floral crowns and men wear crowns of greenery.

what we do. Close relationships that didn't include Wicca had a corner that didn't get filled. Sharing that corner is wonderful and makes the relationship more grounded and whole and more resilient to outside pressures. All relationships need nurturing and work but there definitely is something enriching about a magical partnership."

Dawn: "I was initiated so early that I find it hard to know what I would be like without Wicca. I have had intimate relationships with non-Wiccans but there was always something missing. It is to do with them seeing the Goddess within you and you seeing the God within them. There is a certain respect and excitement to do with the primal dance of the Gods from which everything is continually being born which gives an extra depth to your lovemaking—at times it goes beyond who your partner is and you touch that divine dance of the Gods. You can feel it with a non-Wiccan but you know they don't understand it. Also, priests respect the priestesses. In Craft we train priests well—because of the equality between people we have an equality between us. We often work in circles and you can't let any bad feeling go into that, so you have to sort out difficulties or you would have to cancel the ritual.

Holed stones strung together to protect a house. These good-luck charms are called hag's stones, witch's stones, and lucky stones.

"The Craft is greater than our relationship. You have to step out of your mundane life into this other life very regularly for Sabbats, esbats and meditations, so that creates a pattern. It does give strength to a relationship because there is so much celebration involved. Couples can get so isolated without family nearby. When we meet people outside the Craft they can't

The Craft is greater than our relationship.

believe how many friends of different ages we have. There is something that binds you together. These are people you nurture and care for and with whom you celebrate. We do a lot of self-development, but our group does work magic. We do it sparingly—we only meet once a month. We do look into it deeply and consider the ethics and the worthiness of the magic before we agree to it. The whole group

Dawn and Tony invoke the Goddess and the Horned God in the grove near their house. Invocation can have a life-changing effect.

has to be in total agreement that it is ethically correct before we begin.

"For instance, if a woman wants to become pregnant we find out about the situation with the partner. We want to know that it is a sound relationship and that it had been considered for a while and isn't just a whim. We ask if there is any reason why they shouldn't have children and if they would be good parents. Then we try to find out the medical reasons why they couldn't conceive without help. Often you'll find that there isn't a physical reason, but that the woman has had a miscarriage or an abortion and she put up psychological barriers because she is scared of being pregnant again. We frequently ask for something belonging to the person, like a photograph or a piece of clothing or handwriting, that we can a

Dawn cuts some wheat in preparation for Lugnasah, the festival of harvest. The theme of Lugnasah is transformation through positive sacrifice. Crops must be harvested at their peak. If left too long, ripe becomes rotten. This is true of energy, personal power, and life situations.

link in with. Then we will decide if we are going to use appropriate crystals. We usually try to find something that we can focus the magic into. We send this to the person because a tangible object helps them to focus themselves and to feel stronger and more positive. We may make a talisman or an appropriately shaped God or Goddess symbol, and then as a group we raise energy. We will all be very sure of the intent and send that energy into the object. We may use thought forms, words, or chants, and seal the talisman and send or give it to the people.

"Sometimes we stir things in the cauldron—we put in herbs, crystals, or appropriate essential oils and we will all take turns to stir it while dancing around. We like that focus of the more ancient Craft, which fits in with the rural locale, and that imagery fits us as Witches. Although we are Wiccans, most of us feel we are Witches in that cottagy Witchcraft way—using things from nature and using herbs and stirring cauldrons—rather than talisman making and concentrating on the symbology, which is Wiccan. Many modern

Wiccan ways are more urban. We can go out into a cornfield and cut some corn with a sickle, which makes us feel in touch with the land. We make our own tools rather than buying them, and find plants to make incense, so the incense comes from what is growing around us, and we always use water from a local sacred well in our circles. Usually we will have homemade wines from local fruit. In the autumn we collect leaves that have fallen from the trees to make a circle, which puts us in touch with the seasons. Bringing the outside in feels more Witchy than Wiccan. And we are more likely to use the terms 'lord' and 'lady' than the mythological names for gods and goddesses."

Tony: "We use epithet, simile, and metaphor rather than half-remembered names from mythology that may or may not harmonize with the locality—mythology does grow out of the land. Wicca is defined by and

comes out of a very small tradition passed on from coven to coven. Witchcraft is a very broad and natural thing that our ancestors have done for thousands of years, whereas Wicca has grown and developed over the last 150 years or so. It is continually evolving; it draws on the old and the new and has a kind of elastic orthodoxy. Areas where Witchcraft and Wicca broadly start and finish is about transmission and reception between teachers and pupils, between people who have walked the path before and apprentices."

Dawn: "In the Craft we are not so much at the mercy of life. We know the magic works because we have done it for so many. You can help yourself and influence the forces of life in a positive fashion. It stops you feeling like a victim and makes you feel you have influence. Knowing you can work that magic makes you more confident with life and more experimental."

Corn dollies or brid dolls are fertile charms used to bless a house and represent the Goddess of the land.

PROTECTION SPELL

*I worked this spell to protect a child who was being bullied at school,
a very common occurrence at work and school. You could adapt this spell for
other situations which require protection.*

Work this spell on a waning moon, so the bullying will diminish and stop by the dark of the moon. Collect herbs that have protective qualities. The herbs I used were rosemary, bay, basil, lavender, honeysuckle, peppermint, and rose oil.

Visit a sacred well or spring and collect some water, or buy some bottled spring water.

In your temple, construct a circle of protection, call upon the powers of the four elements, and invite your deities to join you. Drum to raise energy and to ready yourself for the magic.

When you feel imbued with power, place a photograph of the person or a piece of their hair under your cauldron and pour the sacred water into the cauldron. Then sprinkle the herbs one by one into the cauldron, asking each for its energy and qualities to protect the person.

Take your wand and visualize the person surrounded by friends, all laughing together.

Focus this image into the water, plunge your wand into the water and begin stirring a circle of protection around the person. Finish with words to seal the spell.

Bless some cakes and wine, and sit quietly until you are ready to close your circle.

Leave the herbs in the water all night. Next day strain and bottle the water, and advise the person to pour a little into their morning bath. If a child, tell them that it is special water to stop them being bullied.

Dawn collects sacred water from St Winifred's Well in Shropshire, England.

JUDY HARROW
WICCAN PSYCHOLOGIST

Judy Harrow is a retired Civil Servant who lives in New Jersey, on the outskirts of New York city. Judy has a masters degree in counseling and her interest in psychology has led her to write about coven management. Issues inevitably arise out of the needs of an intimate community, but few have tackled group dynamics. It is fraught with passions and temperaments. Judy is a soft-spoken elder who advises on many projects and communicates with Witches worldwide via the internet.

She began to study Witchcraft in 1976, and was initiated in 1977. She founded Inwood Study Group in June, 1980. After she received her Third Degree (Gardnerian) in 1980, this group became Proteus Coven. Proteus affiliated with the Covenant of the Goddess (CoG) in 1981. She was the first member of CoG to be legally registered as clergy in New York City in 1985, after a five-year effort requiring the assistance of New York Civil Liberties Union. She founded the Pagan Pastoral Counseling Network in 1982, was the first editor of the Network's publication, and co-created a workshop series on basic counseling skills for coven leaders. This grew into a series of intensive workshops for Pagan elders on a range of topics. Judy is a member of the Executive Board of the New Jersey Association for Spiritual, Ethical and Religious Values in Counseling and of the Steering Committee of the Interfaith Council of Greater New York. She also serves on the Board of Advisors of the Pastoral Counseling Department of Cherry Hill Seminary. She appears on television and radio and has written for magazines and contributed to scholarly books as well as writing *Wicca Covens*.

> Her interest in psychology has led her to write about coven management. Issues inevitably arise out of the needs of an intimate community, but few have tackled group dynamics. It is an area fraught with passions and temperaments.

An effigy of the Crone in the 1999 Glastonbury Goddess Conference. This is one aspect of the Triple Goddess.

The oak is an ancient symbol of the God in nature. The Oak King governs from yule to midsummer.

"I was very predisposed towards the Craft. Even though I grew up in New York, I'd become very nature oriented through going to summer camp, participation in Girl Scouting, and so on. I have always lived within walking distance of one or another large park, always gone to walk or sit under the trees when I needed to find peace or feel my way through some sort of confusion. I was also a pretty vocal feminist even before Betty Friedan's book came out during my second year of college. Plus, I always loved ritual.

"The people I knew who loved and practiced ritual did not share my geo-centric and feminist values. I had no idea that contemporary neo-Paganism existed till I was about thirty years old. I met some Pagans who took me to a Pagan Way Samhain ritual in 1976. It was the classic "Pagan home-coming" experience for me. It was all new to me, and I had no idea what it was all about or how to conduct myself. Early in 1977, the people who

were hosting the Pagan Way announced a beginner's class. I thought it was just that: orientation for new-comers. That's how clueless I was. Actually, it was a pre-initiatory training group. But I was comfortable with the people and drawn to what they were doing, so I stayed and was initiated in September 1977.

"I use the terms Witch and Wiccan interchangeably. They are the same word. In Old English, a double c was pronounced as a ch sound. When I came to the Craft, we used the hard k pronunciation with people we thought might be put off by the word Witch.

"Every culture that I know of that believes magic can make a difference also recognizes the possibility of unethical practice. They all have a word for an evil sorcerer. In Christian culture, it was believed that any magic done outside the sanction and control of the Church was by definition evil. We were condemned for healing and blessing in the wrong names. Then all those other words for evil sorcerers got translated into English as "Witch." The indigenous traditional faithkeepers learned to think of us as bad guys. We, not understanding, helped keep this false impression going.

"We have come to realize that those persecuted for Witchcraft did not practice the same religion we practice today. That was constructed from historical and anthropological research and, I believe, from direct sacred inspiration in the early and middle twentieth century. Most of those who were persecuted and cruelly murdered were Christians, many were unpopular

> ## All the indigenous traditional faithkeepers learned to think of us as the bad guys.

or even weird. Some may have kept some of the customs of folk magic.

"The word 'Witch' in English meant unlicensed sorcerer. No state office issued me a license to work magic, and I don't think any ever will! I am a

Witch in the old sense as well as the new—an unlicensed magician and a consecrated priestess of mother earth.

"Our coven emphasizes nature mysticism, personal creativity, and priestly service. To learn more you are warmly invited to our web site at http://www.draknet.com/proteus.

A simple earth altar created at the foot of an oak tree.

Judy Harrow spends many hours on the internet contacting other Wiccans and weaving together the different traditions.

"I do not see Witchcraft as a separate religion, but as a committed religious order within the neo-Pagan community. Sort of like the difference between being a Franciscan or Jesuit within the Roman Catholic Community. These orders share a deeper level of commitment than even devout Catholic laity. Each of them has its styles of worship, but they are both still Catholics and recognize each other as such. Similarly with the different Wiccan traditions, and with Druids, Asatruar, and so on. We are all Pagans, and all committed to the Pagan 'religion,' although we may have different patron deities, different styles of worship, different contributions to make to the greater whole.

"So maybe what I have to say applies more to Paganism as a whole. Our religion is becoming more real with every passing year. We are living our lives, and encountering all the normal stresses, joys, and griefs. We are marrying and raising children, burying our parents, aging, getting sick or hurt, celebrating achievements. As our religion guides and supports us through all these normal situations and challenges of life, we discover what tools and resources are needed and we create them. So, for example, *The Pagan Book of Living and Dying*, an anthology edited by Macha Nightmare and Starhawk, provides resources for dealing with death and bereavement, ranging from very practical information to ritual poetry.

"As we follow the cycles, worship together, and live our lives in the light of this religion, we begin to have enough of a pool of common resources to reflect upon, to think about what all this means deep down. We are beginning to develop a real theology of our own, not just trying to answer the theological questions that were raised from an entirely different sensibility. I'm excited by *Pagans and Christians* by Gus DiZerega. It is a thoughtful examination of our similarities and our real differences, and the ultimate complementarity of our paths.

"I think the true path of Witchcraft is that of nature mysticism. This has been implicit all along in our worship of the earth, our placing of her annual cycle at the center of our ritual practice. I'd like to see us deepen that with a real understanding of how her sacred body functions. I'd like to see us live lightly upon her burdened body, in accordance with our values. I'd like to see us take a role as her advocates, protectors, and healers, and to do it from a spiritual base, from our deepest

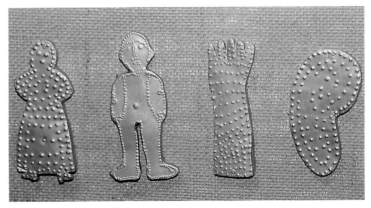

values and strongest convictions.

"I have a degree in counseling. The way this affects my Craft is that I'm very interested in understanding how ritual actually works, how to navigate ritually altered states of consciousness, operational mysticism. My book *Wicca Covens* is a primer on group dynamics for Pagans who lead covens, groves, and other small worship groups. I'm working on a book about spiritual mentoring: how one person can guide another in their development as a Pagan nature mystic, and in living their life congruently with Pagan values and spiritual insights."

Healing charms from the Museum of Witchcraft. To send good intent, create an image of the loved one in thin sheet metal, and then indent it while thinking healing thoughts until the image is covered with designs. It is the focus and concentration of healing thoughts that work the magic into the charm. Charms can be worn or used from afar to heal.

SELF DEDICATION

Find a private place where you feel safe and strong. You may go outdoors, to some natural area. A pristine, untouched spot, however small, is great—but someplace that wild nature has reclaimed and healed might carry some very relevant messages too. So might a garden that you've tended with respectful care for the living earth.

Or do it at home. If you have an art practice, your work area is obviously appropriate. Your bathtub can clearly symbolize a new beginning. If you're working indoors, you can make the space beautiful with flowers or other adornments, candlelight, scent, and music.

Pick a time when you are comfortable in your body. You may want to do this ritual while the moon is new or waxing, to catch her rising energy—wind to your new-opened wings. Consider doing it in the evening. As the seed gestates in the earth and the child in the womb, all new things begin in the nurturant dark. Also, if you do it in the evening, you may find that your dreams carry interesting responses.

Relax. When you are calm and centered, tell the Old Ones that you want to serve them as Witch and Priest/ess. Ask them to guide your preparation for this service, your growth in skill, knowledge, and wisdom.

You may want to dedicate a small object that you can wear unobtrusively or carry in your pocket or purse. Keep this with you at all times, at least until you know more clearly the direction of your growth path. After that, you may want to keep it on a home altar or respectfully return it to nature, in token of your conscious and permanent bond with her.

I recommend blessing a glass of wine or juice, and a few cookies. Share this small feast with the Gods by returning half of it to the earth from which it came and consuming the other half yourself. If you're working indoors, use an offering bowl and bring its contents to your favorite tree soon after your ritual is completed. Remember to give proper thanks to the Gods and bid them farewell as you conclude.

If you don't already have a journal, start one with your description of this ritual, and the feelings and dreams it engenders. If you know how to meditate, do so more regularly. If not, learn how. Pay attention to your dreams. Watch for learning opportunities of all kinds. You have asked for guidance; it is now your responsibility to listen for it. I promise you some interesting surprises. May the Gods bless you as you grow!

PATRICIA KENNEALY MORRISON
SCI-FI AUTHOR MEDIA WITCH

With a history of Second Sight in her Irish-American family, Patricia Kennealy Morrison has been interested in Witchcraft since childhood. One of the most senior Witches in her native New York City, she has been a Celtic Priestess since 1966, when she joined a coven led by a Scottish Presbyterian minister and his wife who had no problem walking both roads—though Patricia is sure their congregation would have.

Her marriage too had a Pagan context: Jim Morrison, lead singer of The Doors, was at the height of his fame when rock critic Patricia met him. The couple became friends, lovers, and in 1970 were married in a handfasting ceremony. After Jim's death in 1971, Patricia found herself unable to run the coven, and the group disbanded.

She later became involved with Margot Adler's Pagan Way, but after joining a Welsh Traditionalist coven and seeing that too disintegrate, she decided to stay away from organized groups. Nowadays, the closest Patricia gets to group work is attending public Solstice services held by her dear friend, fellow priestess, and author, Phyllis Curott.

Patricia's marriage to Jim took place in her New York apartment, and is depicted in the Oliver Stone film *The Doors* (she had a cameo role, performing her own wedding). However, she feels the film viciously misrepresented her, Jim, and their relationship, and also demonized and sensationalized Witchcraft. A professional author, she has written eight science-fantasy books, a book on spirituality, a memoir of her life with Jim, *Strange Days*, and is working on various projects, including short stories, a children's book and a TV series.

Brendan's Lorica
No Sword shall wound
Nor brand shall burn
Nor arrow pierce
Nor sea shall drown

Harm shall come not nigh thee
Ill shall not befall thee
Evil shall not touch thee
Wrath shall never cloud thee

Truth shall ever arm thee
Strength shall ever shield thee
Light shall ever bless thee
Love shall never leave thee.

THIS CAN BE USED AS A GENERAL PRAYER
OR SPECIFICALLY FOR PROTECTION.

Patricia's Goddesses come from many traditions. She had a vision of the Goddess when she was just fifteen, and that started her on her journey into Wicca.

"I have been actively involved in the Craft ever since I was a little girl, though obviously I didn't then know what it was. But like many children I saw stuff the grownups didn't: floating bubbles of energy, people walking on clouds, spirits of water, and mountains and trees. It all seemed natural and normal, so I never thought to mention it, because I thought everybody knew.

"When I was about fifteen, I woke up one night and went to look out my window. A full moon was shining through the branches of the enormous willow tree outside. Then all of a sudden, coming toward me out of the moon was a woman, who walked across the sky and stood upon the tree. I wasn't afraid, only dazzled, and

I felt loved and protected as I never had before. She wore a long gown, and had streaming hair down to her knees; in one hand she carried a lyre, and her other hand was reaching out to me. She had a face of great beauty and sweetness, and she was smiling. I don't remember how I got back to bed.

"The next day I went to the library, and the first book I found fell open to a picture of the Goddess, as Isis. And it was the same woman that I had seen the night before. Needless to say, I was thrilled! So I took the book home and I read it, and next day I was back for more. And I found Robert Graves's *The White Goddess*. I never looked back, and I considered myself a Pagan and a Witch from that day forward.

"In those days, there were no Pagan book stores, no magic shops, no open covens. There was no anything, really. So you had to come at it sideways, the way I did, through folklore and mythology—you had to do a kind of spiritual archaeological dig. When I was twenty, working in New York between college terms, I met a Scottish couple who ran a traditional Celtic coven. They didn't call it a coven; they didn't even call themselves Witches, really. It was just what they did, and what their people before them had done. Anyway, they thought I was promising material, and they took me on to train. I became the Maiden of the coven, and in 1970 I became the High Priestess.

"I met Jim in a private interview in 1969, when I was 22 years old and the editor of *Jazz & Pop* magazine. I had seen him in concert, and as soon as I

> # All of a sudden, coming toward me out of the moon was a woman.

laid eyes on him I knew that we were destined for each other. When we finally did meet, and touched hands for the first time, blue sparks went shooting off in all directions. It doesn't get any more cosmic than that!

"I think one of the attractions I had for him was the fact that I was conversant in mystical matters, things that

he himself was trying to get across on stage and in his poetry. He hadn't been trained for it, not until he met me and I began giving him some basic teachings, but he saw himself as a shaman, the one who goes to the other world and brings back wisdom for the tribe. But what he really found himself enacting was the dynamic of the Sacred King—he became the God, and he married the Goddess, and in the end he met a God's fate.

Patricia holding her ritual sword. The sword can be used to draw the sacred circle, but many witches do this with the athame.

"We were handfasted on 24 June 1970, Midsummer Day in the old calendar. Jim wore an ivy and oak leaf wreath, I had one of roses and peonies. After the circle is cast, the priest and priestess ask who you are

Patricia's athame, or Witch's knife, the true witches' tool. She is wearing Irish heart rings, hers and Jim's marriage rings, on her wedding finger.

A Wiccan handfast, a traditional Witches' wedding, with the altar on the ground. In handfasts the couple's hands are tied together with cords to symbolize their union, hence the name handfast.

and why have you come. You answer together: 'A man and a woman who have come to wed.' Then they ask what is your name and lineage, and you say what your clan or tribal affiliations are; there's a charge that you and your intended declare to one another, and a charge that the priest and the priestess read to you.

"After an offering of bread and wine and water and salt comes the blood mystery, with which a lot of people seem to have a lot of issues. It's

called the *cro-cotaig* in Irish, and it goes back to the dawn of antiquity. There are records of it being used, in the modified form of a pin pricking of the finger, to solemnize contracts as late as the 1950s in Ireland and the Scottish Highlands. So it's obviously something that is deeply embedded in the Celtic psyche: it shows a warrior's willingness to suffer for the beloved, and it's a lot more seriously demonstrative than the 'for richer, for poorer, for better, for worse' stuff other couples promise!

"The vow is, 'The blood of my heart bind thee to me'; you make the tiny cuts with a consecrated athame, you drop a few drops into a chalice of wine and then you drink the wine between you. Hardly rivers of gore! You've sucked more blood out of a paper cut than Jim and I drank that night. But people get completely freaked out when they hear that our wedding involved a couple of drops of blood—I find that tiresome and offensive. I don't trash their wedding traditions, they shouldn't trash mine.

"Then we said our wedding vows and exchanged rings—Irish

claddaghs, a gold one for Jim and a silver one for me, for the God and the Goddess, though Jim thought the silver ring wasn't 'grand enough' and later he gave me an antique diamond band. Then our joined hands were bound with a red silk cord, which

The wall in Patricia's kitchen showing her posters of Jim Morrison. She met him through her connection to the music industry.

usually both sets of parents do for the bridal couple, but that wasn't going to be the case here—Jim had for years been telling people his parents were dead, and my parents would never have understood. More prayers and

blessings, and we stepped over the ritual sword and left the circle as husband and wife."

Early in his career, Jim had assumed the byname 'Lizard King,' and Patricia was now his Queen. Though he may have meant it tongue-in-cheek, Morrison was really tapping into

When he died, I was devastated. It was a complete surprise, a shock.

a major mystery, of which he was only partly unaware. In every pre-Abrahamic spiritual tradition, especially the Celtic, the Sacred King marries the Grail Queen, priestess representative of the Sovereignty of the Goddess. They rule well, but they know that the King must die for the people, while the Queen must continue his work in the world, with him still by her side.

"That is pretty much how we saw our marriage. Whether he knows it or

not, a man whose inner Godhood has been awakened, on any level, seeks the Awakened Goddess to be his mate. That's the person he's looking for, and if he is spiritually aware at all he will know her when he sees her.

"I think the dynamic of the Sacred Marriage, the *hieros gamos*, is at work in every love relationship. But handfasting is the only kind of marriage we have that acknowledges that, in any religion. In olden times, a handfasting was valid for a year and a day, then if you wanted to stay married you renewed the vows. Jim and I did this, obviously, but in our tradition a handfast wedding can be made for any timeframe you choose, and that's what we did. We knew that this was something we had done before, in prior lives, that we were actually renewing vows, not taking new ones. Handfasting is an act of love and faith and commitment without limitation for those who enact it, and it is also a love spell for everyone who can recognize what it is.

"Jim and I were married in this world for thirteen months. When he died, I was devastated. I knew it was coming: he had visited me the night before he died, as the 'fetch the soul traveler.' But I couldn't know what it would feel like until it came; nobody could know. What got me through was knowing that although Jim isn't here physically, he is with me even so. You're still married if your husband is in London and you're in New Hampshire, right? Well, handfasting works the same way. Jim and I are still married—the relationship is simply differently energized. Jim is here all the time; he stays to be with me, because he chooses to. That is how he acts within our marriage; the way I act within our marriage is that I have been faithful to him for thirty years. I don't expect outsiders to understand, really.

"But because of that, I have been able to get through the past thirty years. I'm his wife, not his widow. He's my husband, not my late husband.

Jim Morrison drew this sketch for Patricia. It now hangs on the wall of her New York flat.

An athame created by George Alexander, a famous maker of ritual tools.

He's still in love with me, I'm still in love with him. That won't change."

Patricia Morrison doesn't train people formally, but many have been introduced to Witchcraft and Paganism through her memoir Strange Days *and her science-fantasy series* The Keltiad.

"I consider that I've made the Craft accessible to people who would never read a book about Witchcraft *per se*, but who would read a fantasy novel or a memoir of life with a rock star. It's my way of sneaking round to the back door and then holding it open for them to come inside. I've gotten thousands of letters from people who've read *Strange Days*, and every single one of them says the same thing: they say that how I explain Paganism makes so much sense, they feel drawn to it, their own birth religions have failed them and the Craft seems logical and beautiful. That makes me feel proud and humble, and I am honored that they say so. But I don't feel it's my job to be, in that sense, a teacher. In all modesty, I try to teach by example: this is what I do, here's how it works for me, maybe it'll work for you too. And if that leads

Patricia and Jim Morrison of the Doors were handfasted in this room in Patricia's flat.

people to the Path that's right for them, then I feel I've done my job.

"That's also what I try to do with *The Keltiad*, in a fictional context. It's Kelts in Space, King Arthur meets Star Wars. It's the Celtic ethos taken out to the stars, to a future Celtic realm where cultural imperialism did not intervene, where Pagan values could prevail as they never did on Earth. As a writer, a priestess, a shamaness, I'm connecting my Celtic present to the past of my Celtic forebears and forward into that imagined future. That's also the way Jim saw his music, linking himself to the tribe and the tribe to the gods, through him as a shaman, a poet, a singer and a priest. That's how we see ourselves, as partners and mates, as priestess and priest, as King and Queen. It's how we serve the Goddess and the God—by honoring them with our gifts as they have honored us with theirs."

Patricia's fridge is covered with Pagan stickers and images of Jim.

PHYLLIS CUROTT
HIGH PRIESTESS & NY ATTORNEY

Phyllis Curott is a practicing New York attorney and High Priestess. She has made Wicca her personal journey and has used her skills as a lawyer to bring the rights of Wiccans to the courts. Witches have long needed the protection of the law, as they suffered widespread persecution in Europe and during the infamous Salem Witch trials in America. Now there are attempts to have this spiritual path recognized as a religion in order to gain public acknowledgment. Wicca is one of the fastest growing religions and Phyllis has said that the birth of any new religion is one of the most significant moments in history, as it speaks of the reorganization of cultural identities. She also believes that the rights of those who self-dedicate to the Craft are as valid as those with specific lineages.

She spends her time between her home in Long Island and Manhattan, but recently has felt the urge to move to the countryside. A connection with nature lies at the heart of Wicca, and it must be challenging to practice the Craft amid densely populated skyscrapers. Through her understanding of the power of transformation by intentional thought, she speaks of the potency of balancing the role of women in this spiritual path. She occupies a significant position as someone who can translate law, is a High Priestess, and who worked her way through corporate structures. These different roles make her an important player in world Wicca. Her intelligence and her ability to share the evolution of the Craft with those who would work against it, such as the Christian right wing in America, ensure that the voices of Wiccans will be heard.

She occupies a significant position as someone who can translate law, is a High Priestess, and who worked her way up through corporate structures. These different roles make her an important player in world Wicca.

"A Witch is a person who has learned to pay attention to the sacred. It's somebody who has developed the skills of seeing the sacred in themselves and in other people and in the world around them. It's somebody who has developed the capacity to be in the presence of that deity and to live a life in a sacred manner in a sacred world—that's what a Witch is.

Randel, a Texan Witch, making an offering at the Chalice well, Glastonbury. The Well is visited by Witches fom all over the world and its waters are reputed to have healing powers.

I frequently refer to myself as a "Zen Witch" because there are tremendous similarities between the concepts of contemporary Wicca and Taoism. We live in a world that is vibrantly sacred and alive and a Witch is somebody who is actively participating in that co-creative sacred process of making life and of making beauty, because ultimately that's what life is. Life is beauty.

"A Witch is certainly a servant. A Witch is ultimately a shaman, a teacher, a priest, a priestess—somebody who serves the sacred in whatever ways they're called to do it by the sacred. There's a witch in everybody I know and our job is to call that witch forth into the world—find them and call them forth.

"Part of deity is human and human created, and human interpretation, and part of it is the *genius loci*—the thing that I adore, which is the spirit of the land. You have to work the spirits of place, with the spirits of land. The other answer to what deity is that nature itself is the embodiment of deity. Nature is the gown the goddess puts on in order to be seen. It's the dance the god does to rejoice. It's deity embodied. And so your work varies from place to place. From the Arctic north and the tropical regions to the equator and North America,

There's a witch in everybody I know and our job is to call that witch forth into the world.

what you find is a continuity between all cultures. There are certain core practices, core concepts, and core ideas: that the land is sacred, that there are certain ways of getting to the sacred and experiencing it. You find those similarities wherever you go. There are similar practices the world over: the use of drumming; the use of ecstatic dance, singing, and chanting; the use of a circle; the invocation of deity. These are the core shamanic practices all over the world and they are the ways of being in the presence of the spirits of the land where you are. And then those spirits of the land

teach you how to be in those places. How to be sacred in those sacred places—and that's what we need to do. We need to go back and work with the spirits of the land—that's the message I keep getting over and over again. You can be an urban witch—we are an urban culture—but you have to go back to the land. You have to go back to deity in its most explicit and teaching form. For us nature is the greatest spiritual teacher."

Phyllis Curott (left) met up with Janet Farrar and Gavin Bone while lecturing in New York. A New York attorney, Phyllis has helped legitimize Witchcraft in the United States.

THE REAL POWER THAT MAKES A SPELL WORK

The power that makes a spell work is not to be found in some new recipe book. It's not in the secret ingredient, the ancient inscription, the newest invocation. The real power that makes a spell work dwells within you, and surrounds you: it's the power of your connection to the sacred. The real secret of successful spellcasting, as with all magic, is your connection to divinity, within and without. Your thoughts, willpower, feelings, and physical exertions are actually all expressions or forms of this divine energy, just as air, water, fire, and earth are all forms of divine energy.

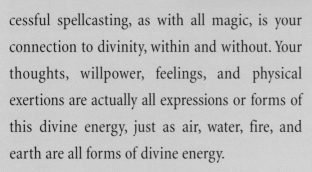

When you understand the true nature of the energy you work with, you can make real magic. When events don't play out as our spell intended, remember that the universe is a complex and living process. Just as humans behave unexpectedly, so too does the universe. Chaos plays a far greater role in reality than we had thought when we viewed the world through the simple mechanics of Newton's laws. But chaos theory has also shown us something else quite amazing: at the furthest fringes of randomness, a pattern emerges. It is the pattern of spirals—the shape of DNA, the building block of life. You live within an organic reality, your life is one of the spirals of beauty emerging from the infinite chaos of the quantum reality. That pattern is your destiny. Some spells advance the pattern, some do not. Those that do often manifest quickly and powerfully. Those that don't simply fizzle, or manifest in unexpected ways that are more appropriate to the pattern of your destiny.

Your destiny is not an unchangeable reality. Instead, it is a probability that requires your participation to come to fruition. A spell, some have suggested, helps change possibilities into probabilities. Wisdom, love, and action advance your destiny. So does being connected to your inner divinity, and to the sacred in the world. The failure of a spell may be filled with as much magic as its fulfillment. When you find the meaning behind a manifestation, or non-manifestation, of a spell, you will find its gift, its magic, and its empowerment, for you are the spell the universe has cast.

THE SPELL FOR LIVING WELL

Go for a walk in nature. Visit your place of power. Then ground, center, and meditate. Look into your heart and ask yourself: What do I want to be happy and fulfilled? Pay attention to any images that appear to you that symbolize your desire and your goal. Thank the genius loci (spirit of the place, or land).

Collect objects that symbolize your goal—you may find them in nature, you may already have them (such as photographs, books, works of art, etcetera), you may acquire something that will help you accomplish your goal such as a briefcase, or a computer.

Write down a simple four-line spell that rhymes and that includes your goal and also the line: "This is the spell for living well." Set up your altar and place your objects and your spell on or near the altar. (Be careful about electronic equipment in circles—the energy has a tendency to affect altars in weird ways!)

Cast your circle. Connect to the divine goddess and god within you and all around you. Then chant your spell as you raise your energy, dancing deosil (clockwise) around your cast circle.

Direct the energy into your object(s) as you continue to chant the spell. Visualize clearly—see yourself living well. Set and release the spell by saying aloud and as loudly as your circumstances permit, preferably with a good shout: "This is my spell for living well. As I do will, so mote it be!"

Ground your energy, offer a libation, give thanks, and close your circle. Act in accord—Live well!

FRANCESCA HOWELL
GUARDIAN OF GAIA

Francesca Ciancimino Howell, M. Phil, has had a glamorous international career combining a number of vocations, from theater and television to environmental campaigning and academia. A native of New York State, Francesca has lived and worked all over the world. Communication skills, writing, performing, and teaching have been particular areas of focus for Francesca, whether as an actress, teacher, environmental activist, or a High Priestess of Wicca. Today Francesca feels privileged to be able to raise her children in the beautiful Rocky Mountains of Colorado.

Francesca's primary interest is in nature. She enjoys hiking, backpacking, running, observing wildlife and other animals, riding horseback, lying on a beach, and gardening. Francesca loves being close to mother Gaia, in all her power, beauty, and fascinating complexity.

As a High Priestess and leader of a coven as well as a mom, Francesca often uses personal interests and hobbies to find sources of growth and inspiration both for her Wiccan initiates and her children. Francesca's first book, *Making Magic with Gaia*, explores the particular path of Wicca she teaches.

A writer and performer since childhood, Francesca admits she is unable to abandon totally her former immersion in the theater and literary world. She says, "It would be hard to renounce that incredibly inspiring background, so rather I look for the sacred and shamanic roots of theater which nourish the ritual work I do now." Today, she works in the Environmental Studies Department in Naropa University.

Evocation to Isis

Hail Great Isis, Star of the Sea!
Teach us Thy magic, unveil Thy mystery.

We are Thy children who humbly await;
Our faith in Thee constant, in Thy powers so great.

As Thou did heal Lord Osiris and mended each ill,
Guide us to heal mightily, through our love, faith and will.

Lead us where our feet should go; teach us all that we should know.

Let us see Thy form and Face; fill us with Thy power and grace;

That we may heal and teach and lead, helping others in their need.

Giver of life, Rhea, Binah, Ge!
Isis unveiled, we call unto Thee.

FRANCESCA CIANCIMINO HOWELL, M.PHIL
HIGH PRIESTESS OF THE TEMPLE OF GAIA

A black scrying mirror and a crystal ball, both tools of divination. This crystal ball belonged to Cecil Williamson, founder of the Museum of Witchcraft.

"I'm an initiate of a tradition that originated in New York. New Yorkers have as much right to a connection with nature as anybody else! My beloved Hudson Valley was where I first connected with nature. I am an initiate of the Gaia Group, and have a daughter coven, The Temple of Gaia. We are an earth-stewardship tradition based in Wicca. The tradition stems from Alexandrian/Gardnerian Wicca with a couple other sources—what I jokingly call 'mainstream Wicca.'

"We are more traditional than many, but we have an overriding focus: as initiates we take vows to serve and heal the earth in whatever way we can. Our guiding ethos is to work on both the mundane plane and the magical or the astral plane. I call this path 'magical deep ecology.' It's very hard to do a ritual about, for example, helping the oceans to be cleaner and healthier and then be very wasteful of water as many Americans are. It makes you live more mindfully, with a great deal more respect for the earth around us.

"It is very important to look at the social and political milieu that one comes from. My initiators, Myrddin and Crystal, were responding to the Cold War era when they created the Gaia Group. They came from two very different traditions of Wicca. One was Welsh, the other a Raymond Buckland tradition—a mix of Gardnerian and Alexandrian Wicca with some High Magical training, too.

In the early 1970s Myrddin and Crystal didn't see a strong ecological consciousness in the Craft on a personal or a magical basis. They broke new ground on the East Coast by taking vows that were deeper and more binding at each initiation towards serving the earth. In our practice, every ritual has some act of earth-healing magic.

"Our work stems from the British tradition in terms of how we cast a circle, use salt and water to cleanse and purify, and so on. We call upon a God and a Goddess to be with us and work with the polarity of male and female. In calling up the quarters we call upon male watchtowers in the east and the south, female in the west and the north. It's traditional, but we have our own take on it.

"My coven is committed to political as well as ecological magic. We also perform High and Low Magic. We don't only work with the 'imported' Gods and Goddesses, but since we're people of European descent, I think it's our birthright to work that way. And being that we are psychic people, telepathic people, magical people in this landscape, we have to connect to the totem animals and nature spirits that are connected to this land and to the ancient American Indian traditions here. However, we come with our own constructs too. And if we're doing magic for Africa, we may work with African deities, if we're doing magic for the Andes, then I call upon Andean deities.

"I started training in Witchcraft with an older girl when I was about ten. She was quite adept in divination, spellcraft, and trancework, and worked with the elementals. I started doing Tarot, I Ching, trancework and past-life regression, and other magic and spent a lot of time in the woods, communing with the spirits and nature.

Francesca Howell using her crystal-tipped wand in the mountain range above Boulder, Colorado

Francesca has been an activist since early childhood and, like Starhawk, she combines politics with magical work.

"I worked with Greenpeace and the Environmental Investigation Agency and I was a lobbyist at the International Whaling Commission in the

I overlap my professional work, my life's work, and my spiritual life.

late 1980s and early 1990s. Starhawk's courage made an enormous impression on politically minded Pagans and Witches everywhere. I didn't read *Spiral Dance* until 1985. By then I had been an activist for over ten years, because I started monkey-wrenching at eleven. This is not a very PC activity: it's vandalism in the name of the environment. But as a young girl, I felt it was one of the few things we could do to express our dismay at the development in the Hudson Valley. That and protests and political campaigning.

"I joined McGovern's campaign when I was about twelve, because he seemed the more environmentally switched on. So from childhood I've been an activist for women's rights, human rights, and particularly animal rights and the environment. As an

adult it was my avocation, my hobby for many years. As I found formal Wicca and Wiccan training, and then found the Gaia Group, I tried to overlap my professional work, my life's work, and my spiritual life. That's part of my vows as a Priestess. Of course, I follow the Wiccan ethic 'Do what thou wilt an' it harms none.' I was a staunch vegetarian for many years and, though I'm not formally a pacifist, I certainly see myself as that.

"We environmentalists are often seen by the right wing and by the

Crystals are cleansed in running water in preparation for a healing ritual.

Francesca in ritual attire. She is using the sword to cast a circle. The use of a sword in Wicca probably derives from ritual magic and freemasonry.

The mesa is a rich source of herbs such as sage, which can be used as incense.

developers as being the eco-terrorists. However, to me, eco-terrorists are the people who are doing these devastating acts and projects that harm mother Gaia. I admire activists of all kinds, but I can never agree with violence.

"In my twenties I lived in Chile under General Pinochet, which was a formative experience. I was a high-profile actress-turned-environmentalist. I was taken in by the Chilean Police one time and I joined the unions although they were outlawed there. I believe in risking one's life for what one believes in. Once I chose to have children I had to shelve that for a time. However, you can do other kinds of political work.

" I wrote *Making Magic with Gaia: Practices to Heal Ourselves and Our Planet* because I believe that spending time in nature and doing magic and ritual—staying connected with Gaia on the deepest levels—keeps the flame bright within you. It helps to keep the macro picture and that's always healthy.

"Gaia is the spirit of the earth. Gaia was the ancient Greek's name for the primordial earth mother. The Gaia concept was brought to international attention by James Lovelock in the 1970s. He hypothesized that the earth must be an intelligent being because of the intricate and elaborate systems that she has to sustain herself as a unique part of the cosmos.

"Gaia has been seen as feminine by the Western mystery tradition, but some American Indian and Japanese

traditions see the earth as masculine. We talk about the nurturing, sustaining, fertile energy of our beautiful planet and to Westerners that is very feminine and maternal. We humans are quick to give things gender. It helps us in understanding divinity or nature, or elemental or angelic beings, although on those levels there is no gender, really.

"Nature is often derided as an out of control, chaotic force, particularly by patriarchal culture. Nature is seen as something to be dominated. We use the concept of 'stewardship,' which implies a responsibility, and has to do with taking care of.

"So I think of the earth as feminine and yet, because I'm a naturalist and an ecologist, I'm quick to admit that nature is 'red in tooth and claw.' The phrase 'web of life' can refer to the incredible web of energy that we magicians work with; its interconnected strands of energy weave us all together. However, it also has to do with the food chain, of which we humans are a part. I honor that in Gaia and in nature. Some of the most powerful goddesses, like Kali and Sekhmet, are the most ferocious.

"We need to get back to our wildness, our primal, visceral instincts. It can be incredibly healing and enlightening and would help us through some of the dark times as well as the good times. Nature is a primal force which can rage and destroy, but can also heal and nurture. When

Francesca using her American Indian rattle to bless plants before gathering them.

An Iroquois rattle used for ceremony, clearing space, and for healing.

Francesca was given her bald-eagle and owl feathers by American Indian healers. She combines her Wiccan training with the traditions of the local area in Colorado.

An owl feather ritual talisman. Feathers are often used to represent the element of air.

Gaia talks to me and guides me, she may grab me by the hair or she may touch me with a gentle kiss."

Like many Americans, Francesca has diverse cultural roots, yet relates directly to the land she finds herself in.

"I'm Irish-American and Italian-American and I grew up spending time in all three countries. I'm named after Saint Francis of Assisi; I was born on his day (4 October). As well as being influenced enormously by my family's Italian roots, I also was influenced by the Irish world and the Celtic fairy tradition, and by that very Mary-oriented brand of Catholicism. When I was a child, my mother taught about talking to trees and watching the fairies dance on the lawn. She would carry any insect out of the house and help any animal. That connects to a key point in magic and in all true spirituality—compassion. Compassion is important in any true path to spiritual evolution.

"When I lived in Latin America I began to sense the ancient forces at work in the Andes mountains with the indigenous cultures. I later studied those cultures in university, and finally began to work with a Native American teacher. His native name is Beautiful Painted Arrow and his Christian name is Joseph Rael.

"There are huge areas of overlap between Wiccan and the American Indian practices and philosophies. I was born in the Hudson Valley, where there is a vital and tangible Indian history. I had encounters with Indian spirits in the woods around my childhood home. When you cast a circle here and you call up the watchtowers, instead of seeing, let's say, British animals, you see buffalo or cougar. In other words, different power animals are drawn to your circle. That's as it should be; these spirits are connected with the land here and they are waiting. Wicca is about the land, and therefore it adapts to the land.

"In my coven we use a couple of techniques of the Plains Indians—we leave an offering of tobacco and cornmeal, long thought sacred in North America, to the land and the elementals. It seems proper to do it here.

"A strong shamanic element runs through our religion, and I love it. It's so important, appropriate, and so rich in learning experiences, whether it's Celtic, South American, Amazonian, or Andean shamanism. In Colorado you can't help but touch that shamanic connection when you meditate and do vision work. The teachers come to you. They are looking for human contact because the earth is in need. These spirits or guides are there to help us find our path to health again.

Francesca often conducts rites of passage for Wiccans and others.

"I have a lot of requests for rites of passage, whether it's over a miscarriage, or death of a family member, a dear pet, or a beloved animal. Sometimes it's a handfasting, or the birth or dedication of a child. People often ask for initiation. I want people to understand that I am only a 'signpost' on the way to help them know that they're on the right path. We don't have gurus in Wicca; we always teach that your best teachers are your inner guides. So I usually want them to go away again and meditate or pray on whatever it is that they need to do. I loan them books and suggest readings. I'll suggest that they get out in nature, walk, do a vision quest, do whatever they need to hear their guides and to contact their inner teachers and divinity. Then we talk more about what it is they want to do. My initiators taught me that when someone can formulate the question, they have the answer already. They just have to be able to conceptualize it and maybe verbalize it.

"So if someone wants to mark a loss, we'll talk about their religious background, because not everyone that comes to me is Wiccan. I try to see what their religious underpinnings and beliefs are and we construct a rite together from that.

"I'll often lead them in pathworking myself, and then we'll define the

> The teachers are looking for human contact because the earth is in need.

rite. Is it to be outside in nature? Should other people or family members be there? Is it a happy occasion, or is it something sombre? I try to be sensitive to who the person is. What is their soul crying out for? In the case of a death, is it closure? If it's a birth or a marriage or a rite of passage for a girl, is it something to celebrate?

"A rite of passage is a huge transformational experience in a person's life. In an initiation, there's an internal death, and a rebirthing. You must be born again to a new life as you work towards greater spiritual evolution. That's why the initiatory path is so hard. I try to prepare my students for the personal upheaval they may experience. Rites of passage are similar to initiation in the mysteries in that in both you make an outward recognition of an internal process.

"Rituals are psychologically as well as spiritually and emotionally important. Acknowledging what we call the 'crone stage,' the time of menopause and of the elder Wise Woman, in a woman's life is such an important ritual. Yet it is disregarded in this society. Thank goodness many com-

munities are bringing that back in Western society. There's also been a rebirth in awareness around these kinds of rites for men. For example, certain rites of passage kept alive in the American Indian tradition have been helpful for many Anglos who have studied with Indian teachers.

"Various organizations in America now do wilderness rites of passage to mark significant transitions. It shows the impact the 'new' therapies such as eco-psychology and eco-therapy are having. In many ways we are coming full circle in Western society."

Francesca performs a ceremony for the earth. The tree was struck with lightning and yet still grows, a testament to the power of nature.

SIRONA KNIGHT
SHAPESHIFTER PRIESTESS

Sirona Knight lives in the Sierra Nevada Foothills of Northern California with her family: Michael, her husband of 26 years, and Skylor, their 10-year-old son, four beagles, and a family of Siamese cats. Sirona's ancestors include James Smithson, founder of the Smithsonian Institute, and she comes from a long line of the Daughters of the Revolution. On her mother's side she is Scottish-Irish, and on her Father's side she is Roman Catholic, second generation Italian, descended from the De Medici. She feels her cultural heritage had a lot to do with her finding the ways of the Goddess. Raised a Catholic, she developed a love of ritual.

She feels her heritage had a lot to do with her finding the ways of the Goddess. On her mother's side she is Scottish-Irish, and on her father's she is Catholic, second generation Italian, descended from the De Medici.

Sirona is a High Priestess of Celtic Druidism. She is also the creator and co-author of the award-winning and best-selling *The Shapeshifter Tarot*. A contributing editor for the international magazine, *Magical Blend*, for over seven years, Sirona makes an effort to keep her finger on the pulse of current events and the growing interest in New Age practices. She also has a special master's degree in stress management from California State University, Sacramento (with honors), and is a hypnotherapist and past-life regression counselor.

Sirona maintains strong Internet visibility (www.sironaknight.com), answering email from fans and chatting on websites across the United States. She also lectures and teaches monthly workshops. She has written several books, including *Dream Magic, The Wiccan Web, The Witch and Wizard Training Guide, Exploring Celtic Druidism, Love, Sex, and Magick,* and *The Shapeshifter Tarot.*

Sirona working with the image of the Horned God. In Wicca the union of the Goddess and the God provides balance and harmony.

"I was raised Catholic. Many of the rituals were in Latin, so as a young girl I fell into the rhythm and syncopation of the words rather than what they actually meant. This put me into an altered state at a very young age.

"At John F. Kennedy University I met someone who said he practiced an authentic Welsh Druid tradition. I went through the initiation and training and became a full-fledged Welsh Druid. The experience helped me understand my connection with the Celtic Druids, beginning my current and unending fascination with everything Celtic. It's something I feel in every cell of my body, probably because of my ancestry.

"The pentacle is a symbol of the Wiccan movement. Some people have the notion that pentacles are related to Satanism, which could not be further from the truth. The idea of a deity representing pure evil is uniquely Christian. Goddess traditions are about making magical patterns. Invoking evil into these patterns would be to condemn them to failure. The pentacle has come to represent a movement of people that are disillusioned by the paternalism of Judaism, Christianity, and Islam.

"I practice magic every day, every moment. Everything, every breath

> **I practice magic every day, every moment. Everything, every breath becomes sacred.**

becomes sacred. I live in the woods, in the midst of oaks, madrones, firs, mountain ash trees, and huge pines. Because of my environment, it's easy to get in touch with the divine at home. Nothing truly dies, but is transformed and reborn, continuing the cycle of the Goddess. We are all a reflection of this cycle. This is the beauty of it all—life, death, and rebirth.

"We are continually transforming and shifting our perceptions and our world. Magic is about having more intention as to how these transformations and shifts occur and more input into where we are going. It's about being a co-creatrix in life, with the divine, with the universe. In theory, there are similarities between these magical practices and the goal-setting techniques used by business people. What sets magic apart is the merging process with the Goddess and God.

"One of the magical works in the *Great Book* of the Gwyddonic Druid tradition is the pentacle. It teaches the student the basics of magical patterning. First of all, you choose a goal you want to achieve. It is advisable to pick something smaller the first time. Then write out the five basic steps you would need to do to make this happen. For example, if you want a new house, see yourself working, getting the money for the house, looking for the best possible house, finding that house, moving in, and living there. Next take each part of these steps and make a symbol for it, such as a circle with your initials to represent you and a house surrounded by a bright star to represent the house. Draw the symbols for the step next to each arm of the pentacle.

"Then use the three eyes of the Goddess to make the pattern happen. The three eyes are: intention, see in your mind exactly what you want to achieve—in this case the five steps of

Sirona in her native woods with her ceremonial drum. She finds it easy to get in touch with the divine in the wilderness.

Creating an earth altar with crystals and the sheela-na-gig, *an image of female sexuality. They are placed on a pentacle, symbol of the element of Earth.*

Dowsing over crystals can help you find the best crystal for your purpose. Wiccans use many methods of divination, including the pendulum.

the pentacle; desire, go deeper into your goal so that you feel it with all your senses; and merging, where you move into the energy of the Goddess, which gives the magical pattern the divine blessings of the Goddess.

"Techniques like the pentacle teach us to take charge of our lives and start patterning for what we want. An essential idea in modern Wicca is that if you truly want something to happen, then there are ways to make it happen. In some circles this is called magic and in others "a" to "b" to "c." What is happening is personal transformation on both a physical and spiritual level.

"Shapeshifting, another method of personal transformation, is a power-

ful tool that ultimately gives you insights into who you are, produces shifts in your life and expands your own boundaries. You can shapeshift into everything, from an animal to a Goddess or a God. As a way to connect with your inner nature, shapeshifting is akin to meditation—a meditation on the relationship between human-kind and nature, especially animals.

"The shamanic art of shapeshifting is based on the idea of assuming a certain creature's characteristics, traits, and talents for a limited time and for a particular purpose. A shape-shifter can change shape at will or under special circumstances.

"Nothing ever truly dies; it merely shifts shape. Everything is continuously reborn, and the elemental components are constantly recycling. For example, if I were to give you a glass of water and ask you to destroy the water, it is impossible. If you pour the water out, it becomes part of whatever you pour it into or onto. If the you allow the water to evaporate, it becomes rain. If you drink it, the water becomes part of your body as well as waste that is recycled into the

Sirona making an offering at a local lake. In nature Sirona feels close to the Goddess.

earth. Nothing can be destroyed (it is ever-beginning, never-ending). Everything transforms or shapeshifts.

"The essence of shapeshifting is merging. Merging is sometimes called 'the thirteenth factor,' where there is no division between body, mind, and spirit. Everything becomes oneness, and all knowledge and wisdom are readily accessible in this place of being, depending upon your intention and desire. You become one with all things. It occurs naturally when you are in the middle of a beautiful forest, watching the sunset at the ocean, or looking into your beloved's eyes.

"When you shapeshift, make your intention specific, simple, and directed. Focus on your intention

before, during, and after merging. Pay close attention to your breath. If you have difficulty merging and moving into the shape you chose to shift into, use deep breathing: for ten breaths, breath in to the count of three, hold your breath for three counts, and exhale for three counts.

"Choose the animal you want to shapeshift with. If you choose to shapeshift into a dog, first spend a great deal of time studying 'dog-ness.' Study their habits, nature, patterns, every aspect of dogs that reflects 'dog-ness.' It helps to have access to a living dog on a regular basis. Pets make great 'familiars' for shapeshifters.

"It doesn't matter if you believe you can shapeshift or not, just let go and pretend you can shift into the animal of your choice. See yourself as pure energy and light, and then project this light into the animal you are working with. Allow the animal's energy to move into you also, like a force field that moves back and forth.

"Pretending and having fun with the shapeshifting process almost always has an immediate positive impact on the results, as suddenly you enter a receptive state of mind. You will know when you are shapeshifting, experientially and energetically, because your view of reality shifts.

"Shapeshifting can bring us closer to nature and animals, so that we begin

Everything becomes oneness, and all knowledge and wisdom are readily accessible in this place of being.

to understand we do not stand apart from nature but are part of it. With every animal that becomes extinct, we lose part of ourselves. Saving species and habitats is crucial to our very existence because they are extensions of our beingness—the richness and diversity of living systems.

"In the traditional tale about a man changing into a golden ass, the man communes with the Goddess, and becomes a better person. Shapeshifting also expands your consciousness and helps you become a better person inwardly and outwardly.

"My garden is a world of my own design, where everything lives in harmony. In the garden, I can most feel the energy of the Goddess, in her many faces from spring and summer to fall and winter. I can feel the essence of life, which is both female and male. It is the oneness produced by the union of the two divine energies

"The union of the Goddess and God is oneness, when the feminine and masculine come together as one divine energy. The relations between the female and male need to improve so they work together as equal parts of the divine. They say in the Craft, "The perfect love of the Goddess, and the perfect peace of the God." This is oneness in its truest form.

The cat is traditionally seen as the Witches' familiar. Shapeshifting allows Witches to see the world from another perspective and to strengthen their connection with nature.

"My garden used to be the summer feasting grounds for the Concow Maidu, a group of Native Americans. I do as many rituals as I can outside, because the hills often seem alive with the energy of those who came before me. I can feel their energy commingle with my energy and the energy of the trees as I do ritual. Often the ritual circle becomes an energetic vortex where all these energies come

The spiritual balance will begin moving to a time when the feminine and masculine come into harmony.

together as one. The experience can be unsettling, but for the most part is exhilarating and continually expands the awareness of my senses.

"I think this is an interesting time to be alive. Technology continues to move at breakneck speed but people are experiencing internal changes that are bringing about changes in our spirituality. For years masculine energy has dominated and people have been very aggressive, but the feminine aspect of the divine is coming back, and the spiritual balance will begin moving to a time when the feminine and masculine come into harmony. The re-emergence of the Goddess, who represents an energy that resides in all of us, is one of the first steps towards this balancing."

Gathering herbs for magic and healing from your local area helps to strengthen your links with the land.

The cauldron is used to mix herbs and represents the womb of the Goddess, or the void. The black mirror is a divination tool and works with crone energy.

BIBLIOGRAPHY

Adler, Margot, *Drawing Down the Moon*,
Beacon Press, Boston, 1979

Baker, Diane, Hill, Anne, and Starhawk,
*Circle Round: Raising Children in Goddess
Traditions*, Bantam Books, NY, 1998

Baker, Marina, *Spells for the Witch in You*,
Kyle Cathie Ltd, London 2001

Crowley, Vivianne, Wicca: *The Old Religion in
the New Age*, The Aquarian Press,
Harper Collins, London, 1989

Crowley, Vivianne, *Phoenix From the Flame*,
Aquarian Press, Harper Collins,
London, 1994

Curott, Phyllis, *Book of Shadows*,
Broadway Books, NY 1998

Farrar, Janet and Stewart, *Eight Sabbats for
Witches*, Robert Hale Ltd, London, 1979

Farrar, Janet and Stewart, *The Witches' Way*,
Robert Hale Ltd, London,1982

Farrar, Janet and Stewart, *The Witches'
Goddess*, Robert Hale Ltd, London, 1985

Farrar, Janet and Stewart, *The Witches' God*,
Robert Hale Ltd, London, 1987

Farrar, Janet and Stewart, *Spells and How
They Work*, Robert Hale Ltd, London, 1987

Farrar, Janet and Stewart, *The Witches' Bible
Compleat*, Robert Hale Ltd,
London, 1996

Farrar, Janet and Stewart, and Bone,
Gavin,*The Pagan Path*, Phoenix Pub Inc,
Custer, WA, 1995

Farrar, Janet and Stewart, and Bone,
Gavin,*The Healing Craft*, Phoenix Pub Inc,
Custer, WA, USA, 1999

Farrar, Stewart, *What Witches Do*, Peter
Davies, London, 1971

Griffyn, Sally, *Sacred Journey: Stone Circles
and Pagan Paths*, Kyle Cathie Ltd,
London, 2000

Howell, Francesca, *Making Magic with Gaia*,
Red Wheel/Weiser, MA, 2002

Harrow, Judy, *Wicca Covens*, Harper Collins
San Francisco, 1999

Hutton, Ronald, *The Triumph of the Moon:
A History of Modern Pagan Witchcraft*,
Oxford University Press Inc, NY, 1999

Hutton, Ronald, *The Stations of the Sun:
A History of the Ritual Year in Britain*,
Oxford University Press Inc, NY, 1996

Jones, Evan John, with Valiente, Doreen,
Witchcraft: A Tradition Renewed, Hale Ltd,
London, 1990

Knight, Sirona, *The Wiccan Web*,
Kensington/Citadel, 2001

Knight, Sirona, *The Witch and Wizard
Training Guide*, Kensington/Citadel, 2001

Knight, Sirona, *Celtic Traditions*,
Kensington/Citadel, 2000

Knight, Sirona, *The Little Giant Encyclopedia
of Runes*, Sterling, NY, 2000

Knight, Sirona, *Love, Sex, and Magick*,
Kensington/Citadel, 1999

Knight, Sirona, *The Shapeshifter Tarot*,
Llewellyn, 1998

Morgan, Ffiona, *Wild Witches Don't Get the
Blues*, Daughters of the Moon, CA, 1991

Scire (G B Gardner), *High Magic's Aid*,
I H O Books, 1999

Starhawk, *The Fifth Sacred Thing*,
Bantam Doubleday Dell Pub, 1994

Starhawk, *The Spiral Dance*, Harper Collins,
NY, 1979

Starhawk, *Truth or Dare*, Harper Collins,
San Francisco, 1990

Starhawk, *Dreaming the Dark*, Beacon Press,
Mass, 1982

Starhawk, *Walking to Mercury*,
Bantam Doubleday Dell Pub, 1999

Starhawk and Hilary Valentine, *Twelve Wild
Swans*, Harper Collins, San Francisco, 2000

Starhawk and Nightmare, M. Macha,
The Pagan Book of Living and Dying,
Harper Collins San Francisco, 1997

Valiente, Doreen, *Natural Magic*, Phoenix Pub
Inc, Custer, WA, 1985

Valiente, Doreen, *The ABC of Witchcraft
Past and Present*, Phoenix Pub Inc, Custer,
WA, 1969

Valiente, Doreen, *Witchcraft For Tomorrow*,
Phoenix Pub Inc, Custer, WA, 1987

Valiente, Doreen, *The Rebirth of Witchcraft*,
Phoenix Pub Inc, Custer, WA, 1987

WEBSITES

Judy Harrow's website:
www.draknet.com

Janet Farrar's and Gavin Bone's website
includes extensive links and info
about books and Pagan resources:
www.gofree.indigo.ie/~wicca

M. Macha Nightmare's website:
www.machanightmare.com

Pagan Federation UK: www.paganfed.com

Pagan Federation USA: PaganFedUS@aol.com
<mail to:PaganFedUS@aol.com>

Starhawk's website:
www.reclaiming.org/starhawk

The Witches' Voice website, the most
comprehensive Pagan website, with
thousands of links: www.witchvox.com

USEFUL ADDRESSES

SACRED MOON
27 Wyle Cop
Shrewsbury, Shropshire
SY1 1XB, UK
Tel: (44) 01743 352829
Email: Shop@sacredmoon.freeserve.co.uk

BRANWEN'S CAULDRON OF LIGHT
603 Seagaze Drive
Oceanside, CA 92054, USA
Tel: (760) 433 3546
Email: www.branwenscauldron.com

STRANGE BREW
2826 Elmwood Avenue
Kenmore, NY 14217, USA
Tel: (716) 871 0282
www.the cauldron.com

MUSEUM OF WITCHCRAFT
Graham King
Boscastle
Cornwall, PL35 0A, UK
Tel: (44) 01840 250111
museumwitchcraft@aol.com

INDEX